HEARTLESS

INTERSTELLAR BRIDES® PROGRAM: PRIMAL MATES
BOOK 1

GRACE GOODWIN

HEARTLESS
Copyright © 2023 by TydByts Media

This book was written by a human and not Artificial Intelligence (A.I.).

This book may not be used to train Artificial Intelligence (A.I.).

Interstellar Brides® is a registered trademark.

All Rights Reserved. No part of this book may be reproduced or transmitted in any form or by any means, electrical, digital or mechanical including but not limited to photocopying, recording, scanning or by any type of data storage and retrieval system without express, written permission from the author.

Published by TydByts Media
Goodwin, Grace
Cover design copyright 2021 by TydByts Media
Images/Photo Credit: Tydbyts Media

Publisher's Note:
This book was written for an adult audience. The book may contain explicit sexual content. Sexual activities included in this book are strictly fantasies intended for adults and any activities or risks taken by fictional characters within the story are neither endorsed nor encouraged by the author or publisher.

SUBSCRIBE TODAY!

PATREON

Hi there! Grace Goodwin here. I am SO excited to invite you into my intense, crazy, sexy, romantic, imagination and the worlds born as a result. From Battlegroup Karter to The Colony and on behalf of the entire Coalition Fleet of Planets, I welcome you! Visit my Patreon page for additional bonus content, sneak peaks, and insider information on upcoming books as well as the opportunity to receive NEW RELEASE BOOKS before anyone else! See you there! ~ Grace

Grace's PATREON: https://www.patreon.com/gracegoodwin

GET A FREE BOOK!

JOIN MY MAILING LIST TO STAY INFORMED OF NEW RELEASES, FREE BOOKS, SPECIAL PRICES AND OTHER AUTHOR GIVEAWAYS.

http://freescifiromance.com

FIND YOUR INTERSTELLAR MATCH!

YOUR mate is out there. Take the test today and discover your perfect match. Are you ready for a sexy alien mate (or two)?

VOLUNTEER NOW!
interstellarbridesprogram.com

1

Willow Baylor, Prillon Prime, The Capital

"Congratulations, Willow. It's a ninety-nine percent match." My dearest friend, Makayla, squeezed me one more time as I waited for my turn to transport. "I am so happy for you."

"Thank you. I can't believe it. I'm---numb." What my friend didn't realize was I meant that quite literally. I should be excited. Smiling. Excitement should be bubbling through me like champagne fizz in my veins. I felt nothing, like I'd been erased.

You're still hiding. Stop pretending you need a big, bad alien to protect you.

Shut up.

I didn't want to talk to the stubborn wench who lived inside my head—a.k.a., the *old* me. The me from a former life. She'd been in charge *before* I'd been kidnapped by aliens and lived through a literal hell. I didn't want to be her again. She got into trouble. *She* made stupid choices.

The new me was doing just fine. Better than fine, I had a matched mate!

The warden who administered my bride testing had already given me a run down on final instructions for transport. I was ready to go. I'd said goodbye to my friends, all of them women from the sanctuary who, like me, had been rescued from that Hive prison.

I was being allowed to take a few personal items with me to my new home—and my new mates. I knew it was a break in Brides' Program protocol. Perhaps Prime Nial and the others assumed we'd been through enough trauma already. They had done everything in their power to make us feel at home her on Prillon Prime, to help us heal. Danika Arcas, a human woman mated to a couple of warriors, was always available. She was in charge of the place and took care of anything and everything we needed. What she couldn't get for us, Queen Jessica—another human out here in space—would handle. The exceptions made for us regarding transport protocols weren't huge, but hugely important. As was our unfettered access to the S-Gen machines.

Leaving our sanctuary was hard enough already. It was a relief to know I wasn't going empty-handed, and I wasn't arriving *naked*.

As if. So humiliating.

A small suitcase filled with personal items had been carefully placed on the transport pad. In just a few minutes I would be on my way to my powerful, protective, and possessive new Prillon mate. *And his second.* Yes, please. I had never been with two lovers before, but the idea of having two experienced warriors completely obsessed with caring for me, protecting me and ensuring physical pleasure? Wonderful. I couldn't wait to find out who my mate had chosen as his second—and mine.

"I wish your mate was here, on Prillon Prime, but he will have to retire eventually. Right?" Makayla's voice cracked like she was fighting off tears—and losing. She squeezed me so tightly I was afraid she would crack a rib. I hugged back just as hard. She, too, had been to hell and back. Maybe I should be crying with her, but I didn't feel sad.

About time.

I ignored the self-talk. I was relieved to be leaving this place, ready to move on. I was tired of waking up alone every night, tangled in my sheets. I wanted a warrior—or two—next to me, around me, holding me, touching me. I needed fire in my veins, where for so long now there had been nothing but ice.

I kissed Makayla on the cheek. "Maybe we'll be neighbors one day, here in the capital." Better if my mates retired to Prillon Prime in a few years, rather than being killed in the war. I didn't want to be a widow.

Makayla released me and we stared into one another's eyes, sharing secrets without saying a word, as only best friends can. Finally, Makayla shrugged. "You know I don't trust that computer. I don't see how it can know who you will fall in love with."

"Don't worry. I'll be happy." I smiled because even as I spoke the words, I realized they were true. I'd met so many honorable—and sexy—Prillon males on this planet, I couldn't wait to have a couple warriors of my own.

"Always the optimist. What if you didn't get a match? Or had to go to Rogue 5?" Makayla asked.

"Wouldn't happen." Those scary jerks with fangs had kidnapped us from Earth, shoved us on a dingy, cold ship, and off-loaded us into our new prison without a hint of conscience. If I had my way, their stupid planet—and that moon they lived on—would already be blown to bits.

Now you're talking...

I told you to shut up.

I squeezed Makayla's hand to reassure her. "The matching protocols would not put me with one of those wanna-be, vampire criminals. I would want to hit him with a baseball bat *while* he was sleeping, not sleep *with* him."

"They aren't vampires. Those fangs put stuff *into* their mates' bodies. They don't suck blood out." Makayla sounded...intrigued by the idea. Was she insane?

"Don't care. Fangs are too gross for me, and I like people who obey the law." I'd had enough chaos to last a lifetime. What I craved was order and routine, knowing exactly what was going on around me and what tomorrow would bring. Steady. Predictable.

Boring. You hate boring.

I ignored her.

Certainty was wonderful. I *knew* my new mates would be eager to sweep me off my feet and into their arms. They would definitely *not* be boring. My mates would be hot. Sexy. I wanted them to take one look at me and barely be able to keep their hands to themselves, so I'd dressed up today, pulled out all the stops.

I had on a gorgeous dress made from a Prillon fabric that was unlike anything we had on Earth. Like velvet and silk had a textile baby. The gown was a dark, stormy blue. Fitted bodice, long, elegant skirt. My eyes were the exact shade of blue to match. Really made my eyes pop. So did the sapphire and silver necklace and earrings I wore. On Earth, this dress and jewelry combo would probably cost tens of thousands of dollars. Out here? It was just atoms and molecules made of random energy. The little electrons

—or whatever—floated around in space until they were locked into shape by the aliens' Spontaneous Matter Generators, or S-Gen machines. Those machines created anything I could think to ask for, from diamonds to lasagna, out of thin air. At least that's what it looked like to me.

I didn't care about the science behind it, I only cared that it worked.

I loved the bright silver, glittery polish I'd painted on my nails. The matching blue ribbon braided into my long, blonde hair. I looked like a princess. Every. Day. Because I could, and because it made me feel royal. Watched over. Untouchable.

Like you're not a threat. Like you need protecting.

I do.

Inner me snorted in disagreement. I ignored her. I was very, very good at ignoring her.

I'd been through enough—horror—to last a lifetime. Moping around, wearing black and feeling sorry for myself was not my style. At first, after the rescue, dressing up had been a coping mechanism. Now, looking like I'd stepped out of a fashion magazine was simply part of my life.

Especially today. I was going to meet my matched mate, the alien of my dreams, the one I was destined to spend the rest of my life with. And his second. My *second* mate. I wanted them to take one look at me and *want* me. I'd heard these alien males when they acted all growly and protective. I'd met Queen Jessica and her two huge, scary mates, Prime Nial and a scarred, frightening warrior named Ander—who I secretly thought was the sexiest damn warrior I'd ever seen. So freaking *big* and *scary*.

No one would dare threaten the queen, not with those two—and an entire planet of warriors—to protect her. Now that I'd been matched, I was officially a citizen of Prillon Prime. The whole planet of vicious fighters was mine, too.

And, hopefully, in a matter of hours, I would have this gorgeous gown literally torn off my body in a wild display of uncontrollable lust, by both my mates. *At the same time.* Two of them. I'd be pressed between them, filled to bursting with two huge cocks, riding wave after wave of orgasmic delight.

It was *soooooo* insanely hot to imagine. Incredible, and naughty. I wanted both of them right *now*.

I still couldn't believe it. I'd actually been matched to a Prillon warrior. Officially matched by the Interstellar Brides processing protocols. My new mate was still fighting, out in space. On a ship. He was a *commander*.

He would be even more powerful and dominant than other warriors. Perhaps one of my mates would be bossy, and the other gentle? Or both perfect gentlemen, until we took our clothes off? Maybe they would demand sex every night? Or every morning? Both? Oh my god. *Yes.*

Two mates.

The bride testing—a simulation of some kind—was sensual, to say the least. Somehow, the alien computer made one feel like every touch, every word, sound and feeling was *real*. An erotic image from the sexual vision I'd just experienced filled my mind. A shiver of raw lust moved through me and landed in my still throbbing core. I was still wet. The orgasm I'd had at the end of the test only made me hungry for more. The Prillon mating collars—and the psychic link they created between mates—took normal lust and turned the volume up to eleven. I would feel my desire, and my mates'—at the same time.

Oh, heck yes. I was ready for lots of mind-blowing private time with *two* hot mates. *Sooooo,* ready. To be fucked. Adored. Protected and cared for. Anything I needed, they would provide. They would *know* what I wanted because we would all three be linked.

Two Prillon warriors totally devoted to me—in life, and *in bed*? So very, very naughty. I squirmed, just a bit. I couldn't keep the restless need from escaping. I hadn't been touched by a man in so long. I tried to recall the last time—before the—before that. I could barely remember my last date with a human man, it had been years.

"The transport window is closing, my lady. If we wait much longer, I will need to delay your departure." The Prillon warrior in control of the transport pad interrupted Makayla's long goodbye.

"Of course. So sorry." I gave Makayla one final, super-tight hug, and walked up the few stairs to join my soon-to-be transported suitcase so we could be flung across the galaxy.

The officer nodded, his large hands moving competently over the controls.

Would my mates touch me with that level of intense concentration?

Were their hands that big? That skilled?

What was *wrong* with me? I was thinking like a horny teenager.

"Are you ready, my lady?" The transport officer had kind eyes. He knew where I was going. And why. I nodded.

Makayla waved good-bye as the hum of the transport pad rose from the floor like an electricity bath. The extra energy building up for my jump through space made me squirm like a shelter puppy about to be released from its cage. *Finally free.*

Oh, yes. I was ready to meet my new mate.

Commander Zarren Helion.

Even his name sounded formidable.

I just *knew* he was going to be one hundred percent *perfect*.

Commander Zarren Helion, Intelligence Core, Black Fleet, Sector 438

The Prillon warrior sitting before me bled from multiple wounds, none fatal, each strategically placed to inflict maximum pain. Lieutenant Oberon Arcas of Prillon Prime was one stubborn fucking warrior.

I have to break him.

I'd tracked him down, taken his ship, and captured him for one reason: information. I needed to know where this traitor intended to go inside Hive controlled space. Who he had made arrangements with to help him get there. More important than either of those things, how he'd acquired the detailed map and technical schematics of a Hive stronghold that wasn't on any of our star charts. Why it was printed, ink on paper, of all fucking things?

The Interstellar Coalition of Planets hadn't used paper to store data in... how long? I wasn't sure. A millennia?

Either he was working directly with the enemy, or he'd paid for them, bought them from someone with contacts *inside* the Hive. Someone behind enemy lines.

"Who gave you the plans?" He was going to tell me e*xactly* where that Hive base was located, and *how* he knew the facility existed at all.

Information even I, leader of all Coalition's intelligence operations, did not have....

"Fuck you, Helion. We've already had this conversation."

"Who gave them to you? How much did you pay to acquire them?"

"Give me a ReCon team."

"There is no one to rescue. Where is the Hive base?"

"I'll tell you that after the prisoners have been freed."

"The Hive do not take prisoners, they integrate us into their Hive mind and send us out to kill our own families, our own people. You know this, Arcas. Whatever prisoners were taken are already dead." Apparently, some warriors had trouble listening, or accepting the truth. "I know you want to believe she's still alive, but I assure you, she is gone from this life. I'm sorry, but you must accept the truth."

"I don't trust you, or your Hunters."

"My best Hunter searched for over a month. She's dead, Oberon."

"Give me a ReCon team. When I've seen for myself, I'll give you exact coordinates and you can blast the place out of existence. That's what you want, isn't it? To turn the Hive into ash and dust?"

I did want that. If I'd missed a threat of this magnitude, another hidden base, what else did I not know about? How many bases did the Hive had scattered throughout Coalition space? A Hive installation like this one could wipe out an entire star system in a matter of weeks. Millions, perhaps billions of civilian lives were at risk, and it was *my* job to protect them.

Fuck this asshole and his refusal to cooperate. He thought he knew what I wanted. He had no fucking clue. I was a warrior who learned from his mistakes. A Prillon male who would do anything to protect his people, no matter how vile the task. *Anything.*

I nodded to Doctor Mersan where he stood next to our prisoner's shoulder. A Prillon warrior, like me, he served the

I.C. now. Like Mersan, I, too, trained as a doctor first. I had long since given up using my skills for anything other than hunting and killing as many Coalition enemies as possible. Threats from within or without, I hunted them down. My entire being focused on one task, one goal: ending this fucking war.

Mersan stepped close to Oberon and raised the RGR device he held to the prisoner's chest. He activated the small wand. Normally used to heal, my team had made very deliberate, specific modifications to the programming of the standard ReGen wand.

I watched, impatient, as Oberon's skin dissolved, the cells separating from the traitor's muscles laying beneath. The resulting bloody ooze slid down over his abdomen like melted wax, leaving a raw wound the size of my palm.

I preferred not to take things this far, but we'd been interrogating the warrior for weeks. Sleep deprivation. Beatings. Nothing to eat and just enough water to keep him alive. We injected him with medications specifically designed to break his mind. Loosen his tongue. Still, he gave us nothing. Not one fucking bit of useful information.

I supposed his fortitude could be attributed to the Arcas bloodline. This traitor's cousin—Thomar—had not only survived Hive integration but broken free of Hive mind control. *On his own.* Something previously believed impossible. No one resisted the Hive, other than Atlan warlords. Most Atlans died before the Hive could gain control of the massive fighter that dwelled within their males.

Thank the gods. Atlan beasts were feared on the battlefield *without* the added strength and speed Hive implanted technology would give them.

My prisoner was no Atlan. He was a Prillon warrior, through and through. The Arcas bloodline had been restored to its rightful place on our home planet. His family was one of the oldest in our records. Noble. Fierce. Before the system of Prime rule, this traitor's ancestors had been kings.

I stood quietly, waiting for Oberon to respond to the loss of his flesh. It would heal quickly. But this fucker needed to suffer for a few minutes. *Somehow*, this Prillon had access to information I did not. Vital information about our enemies. Information I would kill to acquire. If Oberon did not break soon, there were other, more aggressive measures to be taken.

Just two months ago, Oberon had been a loyal warrior, a vital part of the Coalition Fleet. According to his military record, he was an excellent pilot and calm under fire. His battle statistics were impressive. He'd received multiple commendations. If I'd seen his record before, I would have considered recruiting him to serve in the I.C. He'd been the perfect soldier.

What fucking changed?

Sentiment. Emotion overruling reason. Love made him weak.

I glanced at Mersan, who nodded in response to my unspoken question. The wound had been open long enough. We didn't want our prisoner to go into shock. Nor did we want to give him enough time to adapt to the pain. His agony needed to be fresh. I gave a nearly imperceptible dip of my chin. The doctor reversed the energy field of the RGR—turning it back to its original purpose—healing wounds, not causing them.

Mersan held the RGR over the wound. The skin surrounding the exposed muscle activated at once, wiggling across the gap, creating new skin cells until Oberon's golden brown chest looked like it never had a scratch.

I watched. I waited. Nothing but impatience flooded my system. This was one more duty I must perform. A job. One on a long list. Nothing more and nothing less. I didn't have time to second guess my decisions. Delays cost lives. Oberon's refusal to cooperate could kill.

Oberon lifted his striking yellow yes to stare at me, one brow lifted in a silent taunt. "You can burn all the skin from my bones, Helion. I don't fucking care. I'm going after her."

"You are chasing a ghost. Continue, Doctor."

Mersan deftly melted the skin from Oberon's left leg. Long minutes passed. My prisoner didn't say a word. I sighed. Time to heal him and repeat the entire process.

Perhaps we should apply the device to Oberon's cock. That would loosen his fucking tongue.

The door behind me slid open.

"Commander?"

I turned around to acknowledge the Elite Hunter I'd assigned to guard the door—and prevent interruption. "I asked not to be disturbed."

"Of course, sir. My apologies. But there is an urgent message from the transport room. One I do not believe you would want to miss."

"What is it?" If the bureaucrats' idea of urgent was another overlong political update, or a Coalition brief on battleship deployments, I didn't want to hear it. Of all the worlds we protected, who the fuck did the citizens think *gave* the leader of the entire Coalition Fleet that information?

"It's from Prillon Prime, sir. From the capital."

Prime Nial then. Asking for yet another favor? No. Not asking. Demanding. Two beings alive had the right to my immediate attention: one, a female I had wronged beyond all redemption, the other, the leader of my home planet. I wouldn't ignore Prime Nial. He was the one Prillon with enough power to fuck up my entire life's work. One word from him could dissolve the Intelligence Core completely. Retire the program. He wasn't a politician, he'd been a warrior first. Taken and tortured by the Hive. Integrated. He'd survived. That alone earned him my respect. "Very well. What is it?"

The male stepped inside and held out a small tablet. He knew better than to say anything of import to me in front of a prisoner.

I glanced down, expecting to see a short, brief message asking for gods only knew what *this time*.

Instead, there was one word from the Prime, and a bit of data from the transport network the Coalition used to travel long distances.

CONGRATULATIONS.

Transport immediately. Interstellar Bride Willow Baylor. Human. Earth.

Matched Mate: Commander Zarren Helion

WHAT. THE. FUCK. "THIS IS A MISTAKE." I handed the tablet back. I looked up to see Oberon Arcas watching me, his expression calm. He didn't so much as flinch as Doctor Mersan dissolved an ever larger area of skin from his back and shoulder. Fucking stubborn Prillon. He refused to accept the truth. My best Hunter, Kayn, had tracked his sister for weeks and felt nothing.

She was dead. Only reason an Elite Everian Hunter couldn't track someone was because they were no longer trackable. No life force. No energy. Gone.

Oberon needed to accept the fact that his beloved sister had been taken by the Hive and those evil fuckers killed her. I needed to destroy the Hive base before they slaughtered any more people under my protection.

He would break. He was going to tell me every fucking secret he had.

"I will be indisposed for quite some time."

Too bad the cocktail of mind-altering substances we'd already given Oberon seemed to have zero effect. Mersan was afraid to give him more. Said it might kill him. Unfortunately, I agreed.

Fucking Arcas family. Too strong for their own good, every damn one.

"And if it's not a mistake, Commander? What should we do when the... *guest* arrives?"

I shrugged. "Make our guest comfortable. Be... accommodating. I will clear up the misunderstanding when I am finished here."

"Is there anyone else who should be notified?" He meant, did I have a second, another Prillon male who had agreed to protect and care for my mate? Prillon warriors always claimed their mate together. In the event one male perished in the war, the second remained to protect and care for their mate and any children.

"No." I had no mate. Wanted none. I was not even in the system. I had not thought to burden another warrior with the solitude of my choice. I had no need of a second, because I would not take a bride, not while the war continued.

"If the guest inquires, sir, how long might you be?"

Mersan healed the skin covering Oberon's back and moved the RGR to the skin of Oberon's thigh. Our prisoner didn't even flinch as nearly a third of his muscles were exposed. Fucking Prillon wasn't even tied down, the lack of bonds irrelevant. He knew there was no way out of this room, let alone off my ship. *My ship. My rules.*

He *would* break. The female bride, whoever she was, wasn't mine. She would have to wait.

"As long as it takes."

2

Willow, Somewhere in Sector 438

THE SMILE nearly fell from my lips as the sharp pain of transport lingered, my entire body tingling and burning, feeling like my foot did when waking up after I'd sat on it for an hour. Not pleasant. Luckily, the sensation didn't last long. Hopefully, I wouldn't need to transport often. Not fun.

"Lady Helion. Welcome aboard."

I gave myself a moment to settle—and make sure I could still move all of my very present and accounted for limbs—before turning to face a large Atlan warlord, covered head to toe in battle armor. I looked around, eager to see *him*. *Them*. My mates.

The Atlan transport officer was the only other person in the room.

Where was my mate? And my second?

Welcome aboard. Lady Helion. His greeting finally registered. "Thank you."

Already I'd been greeted with my new title. This was incredible. Everything except the part where my mate was supposed to be here to greet me and make me feel welcome —and wasn't. "Where is Commander Helion?"

"He sends his apologies, my lady. He is—in a meeting—and cannot leave."

A meeting? Well—he was a commander after all. Important business, running a ship. If it was anything like life on Earth—based on my time on Prillon Prime, politics were politics on every planet—my mate would most likely welcome a reprieve. "That's all right. I'll just pop in and say hello. I promise I won't stay long."

"I—"

I stepped down, off the transport pad, watching the Atlan as he stuttered.

Like he could stop you.

He's huge. He could totally stop me.

Size isn't everything...

"I promise, I'll be in and out." No, I wouldn't stay long at all. I would greet him, hug him and, if I could somehow manage to pull it off, kiss him so he would end his meeting, take me somewhere private—or not, naughty me—and claim me immediately. I was still very aroused from the processing simulation, and waiting made me nervous. Worse than nervous, anxious, nauseous and light-headed. "I assume someone will take my suitcase to our private quarters?"

"Of course, my lady. But—"

"Excellent." I walked to the door, which slid open as I approached. The corridor beyond was small and narrow, much smaller than I'd anticipated for a battleship. Then again, I'd never been on a real one. The shuttle ride to Prillon Prime was a blur I preferred not to remember. I guess I made assumptions based on *Star Trek* episodes. Maybe these ships were built more like submarines. Smaller than I would like, but at least I wasn't an Atlan. Poor guy probably had to duck down and walk sideways everywhere he went.

Speaking of, the warlord followed close behind as I walked through my new home. The walls were barren, mostly gray. Where were the color-coded stripes and segments that would let me know where I was on the ship? I'd studied Prillon ship design, just in case I was matched to a warrior who was still serving out in space. Like my commander.

Green for medical, shades of orange, brown and cream for civilian and family areas, blue for engines and science stuff, red for command and battle zones. There were more, and subtleties in depth of color depending on how close one was to the center of each area of the ship.

Gray. More gray. A bit of metallic black on support beams. Darker gray for the doors we passed. I lifted the front of my dark skirt and looked down at my feet. The floor was black and cold, the thin material of my matching blue slippers not much insulation.

What a strange ship.

When I came to a juncture where my path split into three possible options, I glanced over my shoulder. "Is the commander this way?" I pointed down the branch to my right.

"No, straight ahead, my lady. But I don't think—"

"Thank you." I hoped the floor was clean. I really didn't want to meet my new mate with dirt or grease—whatever kind of filth they had in outer space—ruining the hem of my dress. I hated being dirty. Couldn't tolerate anything on my body or clothing that didn't belong. Not since...

"To confirm, my lady, you are Commander Helion's bride?"

"Of course." I threw a slight frown over my shoulder. "Didn't the bride center send any details about me before I arrived?" I'd seen an imagine of Zarren, back at the testing center, but that had looked more like a mug shot than a portrait. He'd been extremely handsome, but his expression in the picture was severe, as if he were angry.

"Apologies. I do not know. I do not monitor communications."

Suddenly his behavior made a lot more sense. I stopped, turned completely around to face him and held out my hand. "Nice to meet you. I'm Willow."

He stared at my hand for a few seconds before gently—*very gently*—wrapping his entire hand around mine. His hand was huge. The size of a dinner plate. *At least*. I'd met a lot of Prillons, but this was only my second Atlan. Seeing a male that was not Prillon after so many months living on Prillon Prime seemed...strange. "I am Warlord Razmus, my lady."

I smiled, pulled my hand free and resumed walking. "Now we can be friends, Warlord Razmus." Definitely going to call him Raz.

I arrived at a second crossroads. "This way?"

He nodded, but I thought I heard a slight groan come from behind me as we approached yet another male—who was also *not* my mate. He wasn't Prillon, either.

The warlord introduced us. "Elite Hunter Kayn, this is Lady Willow Helion."

Kayn bowed low, then resumed his stance blocking access to a closed door I could see directly behind him. Fascinating. An Elite Everian Hunter. I'd never met one of those before. I'd heard they could move so fast they literally disappeared, too fast for the human eye to track. *And* that they could hunt anyone, anywhere in the universe, just by *thinking* about them. Some kind of quantum field, psychic connection that led them in the right direction, like a psychic bloodhound. They were the Coalition's bounty hunters, FBI and police all in one. That was cool. And terrifying. Hope none of their males had stalker or serial killer inclinations.

Add to the list one more species of alien male I was thankful *not* to be mated to. Fanged criminals and interstellar stalkers. No and no.

He'd be handy to have around. Bet he's better than sniffer dogs.

Don't care.

I blinked a couple times and shook my head to clear it. Enough of that nonsense.

So, what was this Elite Hunter doing standing here all alone, guarding this door? Was he my mate's personal security? Was he watching over the meeting my mate was supposed to be in? Why did they need to post guards inside, on their own ship? That seemed odd.

I turned around and addressed Warlord Razmus. "Are we safe on this ship?"

"Of course, my lady."

Okay. Perhaps my mate—their commander—preferred an overabundance of caution. After everything I managed to live through, I approved.

I would say a quick hello, check out my new mate, hopefully, kiss him, then settle into our personal quarters and wait for him to bring his second so they could strip me naked, fuck my brains out, and make me fall crazy in love.

I had something special packed for my first night with my mates. It had taken me twice as long to create the delicate lingerie as it had to figure out how to make my dress. I couldn't wait to see my mates' faces when I put it on. Or when they *took it off*.

But that was for later. Right now, I wanted to see *my* commander's face. In person. Those stupid digital images never did anyone justice. My mate had looked very handsome—if a bit stern—on the screen. In person? I had no doubt my panties would melt right off the moment he looked at me.

"Is Commander Helion behind that door?"

"Yes, my lady." Kayn looked to the warlord behind me, their gazes locked over my head.

"Wonderful." I lifted a hand to make sure the braid and ribbon I'd put in my hair was still in place. Yes. Still there. I looked my best. "If you'll excuse me, please." Time to get some Prillon lovin' going on.

"My lady?" Kayn did not move aside. He looked confused.

"Kindly step aside, Elite Hunter Kayn. I want to say a quick hello to Commander Helion. Then I will ask one of you to, please, show me to my new quarters."

"Of course, Lady Helion," Warlord Razmus spoke from behind me. "I would be honored to escort you."

"Thank you." I stared at the Everian Hunter, my head titled to the side. Was he obtuse, or just pretending to be? Silence stretched between us. "Did you not hear me? I'd like to meet the commander and I prefer not to wait."

Waiting, wondering, not knowing. These things were an eternal darkness of the soul. Waiting filled my head with all kinds of demons I preferred not to host.

A deep chuckle filled the tight corridor behind me. The warlord was laughing. "I believe Lady Helion ordered you to step aside. As our commander's mate, since we are not in an active military or battle situation, she outranks both of us."

Damn right I did.

"Gods help him." Elite Hunter Kayn turned to the side and pressed his back to the wall. I had just enough room to walk past him without my shoulder brushing his abdomen. Good grief, were all aliens this big? From every planet?

The door slid open and I forced my feet to move forward. If I stopped, I'd get scared. If I got scared, I'd faint. Or puke. Or both. Not the impression I was going for.

"Hello, gentlemen." I sounded pleasant and calm. Win for me.

Two Prillon warriors were directly in my path. A Prillon doctor—wearing green, that's how I knew—knelt next to an injured Prillon warrior who was sitting in a chair. Neither one of them were my Zarren, their hair and skin coloring didn't match the digital image I'd seen of my mate. Still, the poor patient looked like he'd been horribly burned, almost all the skin of his upper arm was gone, revealing a gooey, oozing mess. Poor baby. I would have been a puddle of tears on the floor.

The injured warrior looked... bored.

Luckily, the doctor was healing him up with a ReGen wand, new skin forming even as I watched.

Still, the patient looked terrible. Sick. Like he'd been tortured. He had huge sunken areas under his eyes—wow, golden eyes, like a cat's-- and in his cheeks. His light brown skin appeared starchy and pale, like he'd been lightly dusted with wheat flour. He was covered with small cuts and bruises. His hair was the same rich tone of his skin, several shades darker, as if his skin and hair color had been taken from opposite ends of a paint sampling stick, lightest at one end, darkest at the other. He was naked—*oh yes, he was—*

but I averted my eyes from his—*oh my, that was large*—private area. That didn't stop me from inspecting his skin where it stretched over prominent bones across his shoulders and chest. Had he been starving for days? Weeks? He was so brave. His burn had to hurt like heck, but he didn't make a sound as the doctor tried to help. The warrior's hands rested on top of his thighs. They weren't even clenched into fists.

I looked around. The bed behind him, next to the wall? A disgrace. It looked like solid metal, a surgical table, not fit for sleeping. The chair on which he sat? Also some kind of metal. Had to be hard as a rock. Why would the doctor not even *try* to make his patient more comfortable?

This was my mate's super-important meeting? Even if this injured warrior just came back from a dangerous mission—which would totally explain the way he looked, as well as the numerous injuries—couldn't they wait to debrief him until he wasn't in pain? Let him eat something and take a bath? The cuts and scratches all over him weren't deep, but they hadn't been cleaned up, either. They were crusty and dusty, as my mother used to say. He had to have horrible bruises beneath.

His gaze locked on mine and I froze in place like a deer in headlights. Those eyes. Not yellow. More like the color of honey lit up by sunlight, and focused on me.

I cleared my throat and told my libido to give me a break. The Atlan and the Everian? Not interested. But this strong, fierce, dreamy Prillon warrior?

Soon, I promised myself. Soon I would have my mates in my bed. This one wasn't mine. Not mine. *Not mine.*

But daaaaamn.

Maybe he was Zarren's second? Oh, please, yes. I barely noticed the doctor, but the patient? Hubba hubba. Super sexy, in a *badass-kill-anything-that-moves* kind of way. All those injuries and his expression showed absolutely nothing?

My pussy woke up and stretched like a hunting cat—and she was starving.

Where the hell was my mate?

3

arren Helion

GODS BE DAMNED, this Prillon was fucking tough. A reluctant thread of respect clawed its way through me as I watched Mersan work like a master, melting just enough skin to cause maximum pain while preventing the prisoner from blacking out. We'd been at this for hours. Were we having any effect? As soon as Oberon's flesh was whole, I waited for my prisoner to lift his gaze to mine.

Fucking bastard looked amused.

"Again." I wanted him talking, not dead. I was running out of patience. The subject was sleep deprived, starving, and had enough chemicals floating around in his head to fuck up an Atlan. He had no close family I could threaten. I had no fucking leverage. All I had was pain. More pain. More. Pain.

Perhaps burning the skin from his body wasn't enough. Or perhaps it was time to reconsider melting the fucker's cock. The idea did not appeal, but failure was not an option. Failure meant people would die.

Mersan's expression looked as grim as I felt. He switched the polarity of the ReGen wand back to destructive mode and placed it over Oberon's upper arm. I leaned my back against the wall, right next to the door, crossed my arms and watched. I was so fucking tired of this, all of it. The war. The pain. The responsibility. The guilt.

Guilt kept me going. I'd been soft once, followed my heart instead of my head. Every day I paid for that mistake all over again. Every night, when I closed my eyes, I watched them die, over and over. Every morning that I woke, I hardened my resolve.

They were dead. I was not.

I should be.

I shoved the thought aside. I couldn't live there and function. What I *could* do—what I had been doing—was ensure I never again made the mistake of being too soft. Too careful. I made pragmatic decisions, not hope fueled, nor ruled by emotion. Not ever.

I watched clumps of cells and blood roll down Oberon's arm, past the elbow. Mersan wiped the area with a cloth, the attention paid in stroking the wound an ingenious addition to the torture. So helpful, the doctor.

"Who is helping you?" I asked.

Silence.

"Where is the Hive base?" If I could discover the location of that base, I could use the details Oberon had acquired to ensure the Coalition could destroy it completely, from the inside out. Block all entrances and exits. Make damn sure there were no survivors. Especially not the Nexus unit who must be imbedded there. The base was huge, more like a

Hive city than a military station. I'd never seen anything like it.

Fuck that. I had no idea such places even existed.

Oberon remained silent. Nothing more I could do but wait and watch as Doctor Mersan reversed the action of the ReGen wand—yet again—and began the process of healing him.

The door slid open next to me. I ignored it. No doubt Elite Hunter Kayn was here to bother me with this bride business. Perhaps the female in question had arrived in the transport room. We would make her comfortable and send her on her way.

I didn't have a fucking Interstellar Bride. Didn't want one. The day after my brother's death, all those years ago, I ordered the warden on the ship to delete me from the matching protocol's database. Whatever female had been sent—I had no doubt she would be lovely—was not mine. Would never be mine. I didn't want a fucking mate. One more life to be responsible for? One more person to fail? No. Fuck that. The weight on my shoulders was more than heavy enough without adding an innocent female whose heart I would break. No, not break, destroy.

Like I'd destroyed Catherine's.

"Hello, gentlemen." A female walked into the room. Gods be damned, she was fucking beautiful. Long, golden hair had been pulled back into an intricate braid decorated with ribbon. I immediately wanted to free her hair so I could wrap the strands around my fist and hold her still for my kiss. She had full, ripe breasts, and hips made to cradle a male's body. She wore a floor length dress fit for a queen. Dark blue, it hugged every curve from breast to feet, the fabric clinging to her hips and thighs as she moved. She looked soft *everywhere*.

Both gown and female had no business being on this ship.

Immobilized by shock at her presence, I stared. Her shoulders were bare, the skin smooth. My gaze wandered to the swell of her breasts over the top of her bodice. My cock filled with fire as my mind panicked.

This was my bride? No. This could not be.

I realized a significant amount of time had passed. I glanced at Oberon to find the fucker as transfixed, and shocked, as I. He held her gaze, dared look at her. If there had been a hint of lust or disrespect on his face, I would have killed him and found my answers another way. As he had proven the last few days, when he chose, it was as if his face were carved from stone.

She turned to face me.

Fuck.

Blue eyes the color of gemstones held my gaze without fear. Those eyes wiped every fucking thought from my mind. Every. One.

"Zarren." She smiled at me. She fucking smiled. Why would she do that? How did she know my name? I never used that name. Did she not know who I was? *What* I was? "You are even more handsome in person. I knew you would be." She stepped toward me. I tried to step back, forgot I was already against the wall, and stumbled to the side. Which made her frown, just a little, a tiny burrow appearing between her brows.

Even as I realized this was much more the reaction I was used to, I mourned the loss of that innocent happiness focused on me.

Elite Hunter Kayn stepped into the doorway and looked at me. He shrugged before I could ask. "Lady Helion ordered us to bring her here and allow her entry."

"I see." Fuck. Everyone on this small ship would know by now. Lady Helion. They would all believe she was truly mine. By Prillon law, unless we were in combat or military exercise, she outranked everyone on this ship in domestic matters, except me.

My mate—if indeed that's what she was—placed a hand on my forearm and beamed at me. Gods help me, did this female have zero sense of self-preservation? No one touched me. Ever. The warmth of the female's hand on my arm set off another explosion in my cock. I imagined her hand wrapped around my length, pulling me closer, begging me to take her.

Fuck. No.

Never.

I had the weight of billions of lives on my shoulders, I could not afford to *love* a single one of them. Emotion made my job unbearable.

Still as a statue, I had no idea what to do. I did not touch others. I definitely did not touch small, delicate females, doubly true when they were this beautiful—and breakable.

She should not be touching my arm. She should not trust me not to hurt her. I was not—nor would I ever be—her mate and protector.

No. No fucking mate. This was a mistake. I wasn't even in the system. How had this stunning human female been misled into believing she was mine? I didn't have a second. Never felt the need to ask another warrior to stand with me when I had no intention of needing anyone's help to protect and care for a mate I would never have. This was madness.

Oberon Arcas, the fucking bastard, burst into laughter. I ignored him to focus on Mersan. Perhaps the doctor would have useful advice.

Doctor Mersan watched the entire scene with what

appeared to be complete shock. He looked as uncomfortable as I felt. Not one word passed his lips. Nor Kayn's, nor Warlord Razmus's.

Only my prisoner dared make a sound. He would pay for his laughter later. Once the lady was so far away she could not hear him scream.

Unfortunately, the sound of his amusement drew the female's attention and she spun around to face the other two males in the room. One, my prisoner. The other, Doctor Mersan, a brutal and efficient warrior, equally as dangerous as I.

"You poor thing." She walked to Oberon, placed a hand on his shoulder—she was fucking *touching* him—and deftly took the ReGen wand from Dr. Mersan's hand. Mute, the doctor let go. All three of us seemed to be incapable of doing anything other than waiting to see what the outrageous female would do next.

She leaned to her left and right, looking Oberon over as if searching for more injuries. "I guess the doctor healed the last burn as I came in?" She looked down her nose at Mersan, who still crouched on the floor next to Oberon. Her presence must have locked him in place as well. "Doctor?"

"Uh—yes, my lady." He stood slowly, unbending his hips and knees as if they were made of rusted iron left to the weather. "He has no other injuries."

"I wouldn't say that, but the rest doesn't look too serious." She patted Oberon's newly healed, bare skin. Did she realize her touch... *lingered?* Fuck, now I really wanted to kill him.

She turned to Kayn, who had moved to stand next to Mersan. "This is unacceptable. We will need soft padding for his bed, a soft blanket as well." She looked at Mersan. "Is there an S-Gen machine here?"

"Yes, my lady, but—"

"What's your name?" She asked our prisoner as she waved her hand to cut off Mersan's response. "Never mind, silly me. The S-Gen is right there." She looked pointedly at the device where it had been installed in the corner of the room. The S-Gen machine was operational, but code locked to all but a handful of my most trusted warriors. She would not be able to use it.

She stopped walking and looked directly at Oberon. "Well? You do have a name, don't you?"

"Oberon Arcas, my lady."

"What a lovely name. Don't you agree, Zarren?" She beamed at me as she strolled to the corner and stood before the S-Gen machine. "Tunic and pants, sleeping, sized to Oberon Arcas of Prillon Prime."

"It's locked. You won't be able to—" I didn't get the chance to finish before she lifted the newly generated items from the black and green gridded platform. How had she broken through our security protocols? No one used the S-Gen machines without logging their requests. The unit here? In the interrogation room? There were two warriors on the ship capable of using it, and we were both in the room.

"Oh, yes. Feel how soft these are. Much, much better." She looked up at me, the brightness in her gaze something I had never seen in another living being, of any species. Was this joy? Over such a small thing? Nothing about her made sense. Why would she feel delight over a set of sleeping clothes for a Prillon warrior she had never met?

Was she injured? Perhaps she had been transported here to be treated by Doctor Mersan. Did she have Hive tech integrated in her brain tissue? Was the Hive technology messing with her mental acuity? She seemed healthy—every fuckable curve—but I was not one to judge the effects of Hive tech on the female mind. Mersan, on the other hand, operated a special, experimental unit for the Intelligence Core, implanting Hive devices into our female operatives. We hoped one of the females would be able to get close to a Nexus unit, the leaders of our enemies. It had nearly worked. Once.

Then a fucking Atlan had gone beast and ripped his head off. Such a waste.

The thought of Mersan laying a single finger on this female made me grind my teeth.

She walked to Oberon and handed him the clothing.

"Thank you, my lady." Oberon watched me as he pulled the tunic on over his head. I stared back, thankful to find nothing but confusion in the male's eyes. Relief flooded me as I realized he was not the sort of male to hurt an innocent female, no matter the circumstances he now found himself to be in. Some Prillon instincts were too deeply ingrained to overcome.

Perhaps he did not suffer the Arcas family curse.

Tunic on, Oberon stopped moving, simply held the pants in front of his cock.

Fuck. She'd walked in and seen him naked.

Had she wanted him? Looked at his body, his cock, and imagined him fucking her? Was that why she was being so accommodating? Desire? For Oberon?

Her cheeks blushed a bright pink as she realized why Oberon waited.

She *did* want him.

Why did the thought make me want to melt his cock from his body? Right fucking now?

"Oh, sorry. I'll just...here. I'll turn around so you can put your pants on." She did so, presenting her back to the prisoner. She was vulnerable to him, trusting. Easily within arms' reach of Oberon. The top of her head barely reached my chest, and yet she looked up at me completely without fear. I could not take my eyes off her. Her full breasts peaking above the bodice of the gown, sparkling blue gemstones rested in a bed of sparkling silver in a delicate pendant resting against her skin. The brilliant blue of her eyes cut through me like ice that sent cold claws of lust straight to my cock. The more I stared, the harder my fucking cock became. She should have been intimidated. Frightened.

She stared back, devouring me with her eyes as if I were hers and she couldn't wait to claim me.

Gods be damned. This was not going to end well. She would be hurt when she learned the truth. I could not keep her, even if I desired to do so—which I did *not*. My life was not fit for a mate. A family. Gods forbid, children.

I told my cock to back off, not that the fucker listened. I might have had a fighting chance if I hadn't *smelled* her.

Feminine heat. Desire. A hot, wet pussy. My assessment of her thoughts as she looked at me—*or Oberon?*—had been accurate. She was ready to be stripped bare and claimed. She *wanted* to be taken. Fucked. Pleasured.

I breathed her in and clenched my jaw to keep myself from saying something stupid, offering her something that was not mine to give. She belonged to another. She must. One could not be matched to a mate when not in the system. I was not in the fucking system.

Behind her, Oberon groaned, his nostril's flaring in reaction to the female's desire.

If Mersan had not been standing so close to our prisoner, close enough to protect the female had Oberon decided to move, I would not have been able to cope with the protective rage that pulsed through me.

I could not bring myself to murder Oberon with her watching. A Prillon warrior would protect her from such atrocities, not commit them in front of her.

My possessive rage was a visceral thing, squeezing my chest with pressure so powerful it was as if an explosive had just gone off in the small room.

What the fuck was I going to do now?

4

Zarren Helion

SHE STEPPED CLOSER to the door. Wisely, Kayn stepped aside, but remained in the room. I caught a glimpse of Razmus lurking in the corridor as well. Of course, he would be there. He had been on duty in transport when my—the female arrived.

"Oberon, are you dressed?"

"Yes, my lady. Thank you."

She turned toward him and gifted him with a dazzling smile. "Of course. Anything you need, please let me know."

Oberon opened his mouth to request...something. Mersan dealt a fast, efficient punch to his ribs. I placated the lady, but we would only be pushed so far.

He shut the fuck up.

I nearly sighed in relief when it appeared as if she were about to leave. Instead, she gave orders like an experienced commander. "Razmus, will you be a dear and track down a soft bed and blanket for Oberon. While you're at it, a pillow as well. Kayn, please get him something to eat and drink. Something hearty and delicious. Our warrior is far too thin. And not to embarrass you sir, but you need a bath."

"Indeed, I do." Oberon agreed as Kayn and Razmus both looked up at me, caught in the female's crosshairs as surely as I.

She, however, was glowing. Literally, *glowing* with happiness, her skin and golden hair reflected the light and shined no matter which way she turned. Was she that pleased to have helped one Prillon warrior? Did I dare overrule her and crush such a gentle, guileless heart?

My cock throbbed, growing harder, more painful by the second. This female was walking innocence, walking light. I doubted she had ever seen death or torture. Been exposed to the atrocities of war, or suffered needless pain.

Fuck. I could torture and kill my enemies. But a truly innocent, giving female? No. I had caused females enough pain to last several lifetimes. I would allow my team to carry out her orders. This, I could give her. Perhaps food and some sleep would loosen Oberon's tongue. If not? He would be in better health for what would come tomorrow.

The lady walked out to the corridor. The loss of her presence was like turning off every light in the room.

Oberon looked at me, ice in his golden eyes. His attitude had not changed.

Doctor Mersan shrugged, took his ReGen wand and left. We'd been torturing the traitor for hours. No doubt Mersan was more than ready for a reprieve, as was I, if I were being honest.

I knew Razmus would walk ahead of the lady, protecting her from the front, while Kayn would fall in behind, watching her back.

I walked to the S-Gen machine and quickly confirmed the proper command code locks were still in place. They were. She should not have been able to use it for anything. The fucking thing shouldn't even have turned on.

I would need to take it apart. Now? Yes, now was the perfect time. The work would keep my mind off the ache in my cock. I would order the others to contact the Interstellar Brides' Program and straighten out this mess.

Before I could begin, the lady's head peeked around the doorframe. She looked around the room, the rest of her still in the corridor. She looked right at me.

"Zarren, aren't you coming? I brought something special for you."

Was that blatant invitation in her voice? Gods be damned, did she expect me to claim her, to bare her naked flesh and take her now?

For the space of a heartbeat, nothing mattered as much as finding out what the lady had brought. A gift? For me?

Searching my memories, I could not recall the last time anyone had thought to give me a gift of any kind.

Fuck. Fuck. Fuck.

I was not a saint.

I took two steps toward her. She held out her hand and smiled at me.

"I'm Willow, by the way. Willow Baylor."

"Commander Zarren Helion."

"Oh, I know." She didn't wait for me to decide whether or not to risk touching her. She leaned forward, grabbed my hand and pulled me along behind her as she resumed her journey back the way she'd come.

With one look, I commanded Kayn to remain at his post and secure the prisoner. I would allow my warriors to follow the lady's orders, but that didn't mean the follow through would be quick.

Dangerous, that's what this was. I told myself to let go of her small hand, limit contact. This touching would only encourage her and torment me.

Rarely did I make physical contact with someone I wasn't trying to kill—who was just as intent on ending me. Her touch was warm. Peaceful. I obeyed the slightest tug from her as we followed Warlord Razmus though the ship.

I hated myself more with every step, but couldn't force myself to let go.

5

Willow

O.M.G. Commander Zarren Helion—my mate—was *smoking* hot. The warden had shown me his picture, back on Prillon Prime. Sure, he'd been handsome—if severe—in the image. But in the flesh? He was a tidal wave of raw sexuality and I was drowning.

Drowning in heat like a howling cat. I want some.

For once, inner-me agreed.

He was tall, like all Prillon warriors. That was no surprise. His features more angular than a human man's. His skin was a middle shade among Prillons, not a fair, golden shade, not dark brown or reddish copper. Somewhere in between, like a polished, smoky quartz. His black hair looked so smooth it shimmered and reflected different colors when the light hit. His lips? Full and totally kissable. But it was his catlike eyes that knocked the wind right out of me. Crystal clear, and the most beautiful shade of green I'd ever seen. Not army green or moldy green sludge. No, they were vibrant. Alive. The color of the newest leaves on my grandmother's favorite white rosebush. Every part of him looked to be in tip-top, military condition. Tight. Hard. Strong. His—manly bits—had reacted to my presence. The harder he got, the bigger the bulge in his pants.

Not that I'd looked.

Well, that was obviously a lie. I *totally* looked. After seeing, I totally *wanted*.

Hell yes, give me some of that...

I knew how to be sneaky. Unfortunately, the *Lady of the House*—hint, she lives *downstairs*—had no tact whatsoever. She got hot and wet and started drooling all over herself. I'd put on lovely lace panties beneath my dress. They clung to me now, all damp and irritating.

Not sure how sex was going to go. Holding his hand drew my attention to where our skin touched, the contact like a lighted match, a warning to pay attention or risk being burned. I wanted him to claim me as soon as possible. I didn't want to worry and fret and stress about whether or not he wanted me, or if making love with him would be like the simulation I'd enjoyed at the processing center. Sure, I wanted intimacy. Pleasure. More than anything, I wanted my new life settled and sorted so we could move forward. With Zarren, and his second. Two mates, two big, Prillon warriors all for me. Oh god, yes. They would surround me, utterly and completely own me, and I would feel safe. Desired. Hopefully, if I could get that Prillon mating collar around my neck as soon as possible, I would feel how dedicated they were, protective. Slap that collar on me, mate. I wanted to know what he was feeling. And when I was ready to rip off his clothes and jump on him like a wild woman? Oh, yes, I wanted him to know what I was feeling, too.

Who was his second? He hadn't said. But then, we hadn't talked much either. I wondered if his second would be one of the golden Prillons that looked like lions? Or maybe one of the darkest, the oldest bloodlines, their skin and hair dark as a black cherry tree's bark. Or maybe one of the copper toned warriors, their metallic rust reds and shining copper hair was a possibility as well.

Or light brown with dark brown hair and golden eyes.

I shivered. The anticipation was going to give me a heart attack.

"Here we are." Warlord Razmus bowed his head and walked away, leaving me and Zarren in front of a closed door.

This was it. My new home. My new life. A place where I didn't have to be afraid all the time.

I turned and looked up at my mate. "Are these our quarters?"

"These are the commander's quarters." Gently, he extricated his hand from mine and stepped in front of the door. I'd opened hundreds, if not thousands of doors on Prillon Prime. This one was different. My mate had to press his palm to one scanner and his eye to another. *Then* he added voice recognition to the mix, his deep, rich tone speaking words the NPU—Neural Processing Unit imbedded in bones in my head—didn't translate. The NPU was programmed to instantly translate every language in the Interstellar Coalition of Planets, and a few more that were not even full members, like Earth.

All I heard was gibberish. What was he speaking? A special code?

What did he have locked in his quarters? The secrets of the universe?

Curiosity was going to be the end of me. I couldn't wait to see what his private space looked like. I would know a lot about him the moment I walked in. Was he messy? Clean? Did he like soft, rounded furniture or crisp lines and angles? Did he enjoy art? Or music? So much to discover.

Zarren seemed uptight. Brooding. Everything he did was so edge-lord. The way he'd looked at the other guys in that little medical room? It was like he wanted to kill them—both of them. Apparently, he didn't even like the doctor. Judging by the perma-scowl on Zarren's face every time I glanced his way, Zarren hated that guy.

Maybe my mate was one of those men—aliens—who *pretended* to hate everyone and everything because it made him look macho or cool or whatever. I didn't understand it, but I knew it was a thing some guys did. I didn't buy him hating everyone and everything. I would never be happy with someone like that. If he were that dark on the inside, I would have been matched to someone else.

Or would I?

Don't go there, Willow. Leave it.

Little bit of truth and you run scared?

Jeeez. Shut. Up.

Still, who didn't like Coalition doctors? They weren't like Earth's doctors. Out in space, the doctors could perform miracles. Literal, miracles. I'd seen it on Prillon Prime. There were no quacks making bad diagnoses or botching surgeries. No drug companies holding back cures for profit. Earth had good doctors, and bad. But in the Coalition? Not liking a doctor was akin to not liking—what? Chocolate? A good night's sleep? A sunset?

Everyone loved doctors out in space. Even the kids.

Not my commander.

Was he trying to be mysterious and edgy? Did everyone around here believe he was cold and hard on the inside? Unkind?

I wasn't fooled.

He practically snarled at his crew, but his hand had been gentle, holding mine. I had no doubt once he got his huge cock deep inside me, I'd be a total goner. I had zero resistance to an honorable man and a quality orgasm. At least, that's what I'd decided when I made the choice to be bride tested. I would move forward. I would be taken care of and protected.

I would feel safe. Maybe, if I was lucky, I'd fall in love. But love? That was pretty far down my list of requirements in a mate. Not even top three, the non-negotiables.

Strong. Protective. A heartless, experienced killer.

There were real monsters out there. I needed a mate who could make me feel safe.

What you need is a god damn weapon and to pull your head out of your ass, Willow Winifred Baylor.

I shuddered. I hated my middle name. Great grandmother something or other. Ugh.

The door finally slid aside to allow entrance. Zarren began to speak, stumbled over his words, took a breath and started again. Was he nervous?

How cute.

I lifted a fingertip to his lips and pressed, just enough. "Shhh. I know you weren't expecting me. I'm sure we'll be just fine."

I didn't give him a chance to respond. Instead, I rushed in to see my new home.

The main room was large. The ceilings were taller than I was used to, but warriors were big, so it made sense. The walls and floor were smooth, dark metal of some kind. I assumed the entire spaceship was made out of the same stuff. There was a second, smaller area that broke off into a small nook. Maybe a kitchenette? There was a small S-Gen for food, a counter with a bit of storage above—shelves were empty—and a table with one chair. The table was covered, not with plates or knick-knacks, but with blueprints or engineering designs for something outer-spacey. Whatever the plans were for, the technical drawings and details were stacked one on top of another more than a few pages thick.

I didn't know Prillons still used paper. Never seen that in outer space before.

Just off to the side of the nook was a bathroom exactly like those on Prillon Prime. I knew how to work everything there. Next to that, an open door that led to the bedroom.

I tried to make sense of what I was seeing.

Surely, this was not where he lived?

He's even more pathetic than you are. Get a houseplant or something.

Shut the fuck up. Seriously.

I'd had enough of arguing with myself for one day, thank you very much.

The dark bedroom beckoned. I walked to the open door and stepped inside.

No. This was not his home. It couldn't be. I stood in the doorway and inspected both spaces in turn.

The large room—I assumed it was meant to be some kind of family room for gathering or relaxing—was empty. Walls. Floor. Ceiling. Not one chair to sit on or cushion beckoned. Not a rug on the floor or single piece of art on the wall. No color at all. Metallic black. *Nothing.*

His bedroom was nearly as bad. One bed, clearly meant to hold him and no one else. Sure, it was a bit larger than a super-XL twin bed one could find in most college dorms, there wasn't much to look at. The bed had one pillow, a sheet to lay on and a thin blanket that had been shoved into a disorganized lump near the bottom.

My mate didn't make his bed.

Slowly, I turned and looked at everything again. Other than the mess of technical drawings on the table, and the single chair I assumed he sat in while he looked them over, the entire living area was empty. He didn't even have an extra pair of boots on the floor, or an extra blanket. His bedding was the only item in the entire space that had any softness at all. Sheet, pillow and blanket were black.

Black.

I thought about switching them to white, but compared to the metallic, boxlike room surrounding them, they would be a candle trying to hold back an underground cave's worth of darkness.

"Your sheets are black."

"Tactical advantage in the event the ship is boarded."

I tried to imagine him hiding beneath the covers like a frightened four-year-old and just couldn't do it.

"This is where you live?" I tried not to sound as shocked as I felt. Not just shocked, chilled to the bone. That bed was *not* for the kind of *playing* I wanted to do. I doubted it would hold two of us, let alone three. Was this how he chose to live? Or was this place a temporary housing assignment? Or maybe a brand new space and he hadn't had time to settle in? Maybe he was out on a mission, and this was a temporary sleeping arrangement.

"Yes."

There should have been fluffy rugs scattered around the

room, and pillows, and comfy sofas to curl up in and read a book. He should have a big, soft bed, big enough for three. The place was bleak. Downright depressing.

I turned to find Zarren watching me, his eyes empty, giving nothing away.

6

Willow

"How long have you lived here?" Judging by the state of things, and the lack of, well, everything, I expected him to tell me he'd been here a few weeks at most.

"Seven years."

"Here, in these two rooms?"

"Yes."

Oh. My. God.

"Why?" Good job. Voice neutral. No shouting. I was very proud of that. Perhaps I should have been more specific. However, the question was multi-layered. Why had he lived here for so long? Why hadn't he made this space into a home? Why was he living like this when he had a functional S-Gen unit, with virtually no limit to what it could create? Why?

"Because this is my ship. This is where I am, most of the time."

"I see." If ever a man—or alien—needed a woman's touch, this was it.

You think he's going to take care of you? He can't even take care of himself.

Yeah? Well, he's not the only one.

"Are you going to introduce me to your second?"

"No."

"Why not?"

"I don't have a second."

Well, that was interesting, but temporary, I was sure. Couldn't worry about that right now. I had priorities. I walked over to the table, glanced down at the array of blueprints and turned full circle.

My skirt caught the edge of the pile of paper, the fluttering of falling paper my first hint that something was happening.

"Fuck." Zarren raced to the table and slammed his hands down on the remaining pages to keep them in place.

The rest rained down around my feet in a blizzard of paper.

"I'm sorry." I lifted a few pages from the floor and tried to sort them into a semblance of order. I'd taken a mechanical drafting class, back in High School. Curiosity got the better of me as I looked at the plans. Looked like three levels, with some kind of power generator on the top. A lot of different sized spaces, but a series of uniform rooms on the top two floors made the place look like a dormitory—or a prison. I'd need to look closer to determine which.

I reached for another page. Zarren was there first, his hand blocking mine before I could take hold of the paper. "These are not for you."

His terse tone irritated me no end. I'd been nice and accepting. I'd ignored the fact that he hadn't bothered to meet me in transport—like a good mate should—and given him the benefit of the doubt about not liking doctors.

"You are very rude."

He froze, glaring down at me—way, way down—as if I'd slapped him across the face. "I am protecting you."

Is this what you had in mind? Super dangerous paper?

She/I had a point. "From what? Paper?"

He closed his eyes and shook his head, mumbling a Prillon curse under his breath. "From yourself. You shouldn't be here. This is a mistake."

I reached out to touch his shoulder but he jerked out of reach like my very presence disgusted him.

Oh, no, he didn't...

"What, exactly, is the problem here?"

"My life is not suitable for a female. Go home. I don't want a mate. Get out of here, before it's too late." He stared down at his hands where he had them spread out, palms flat on top of the table.

The gruff order shocked me to the core, a wave of hurt rolling through me like thunder, followed immediately by anger. How dare he? All of this, from the moment I'd arrived? I'd been kind and accepting. I hadn't asked too many questions or judged him for his austere home. I hadn't even expected him to love me—not that I'd told him that—but it was true. Yet, he refused to introduce me to his second —I didn't believe his lie about not having one for a moment —and rudely ordered me to leave?

How. Dare. He?

Finally getting your spine back, woman? Tell him to fuck off.

No. That was not what I wanted. I wanted to be adored. Sexed up. Loved.

Calling on every tiny shard of willpower that I'd honed to diamond hardness in Nexus 5's lab from hell, I kept my face blank as I stood my ground. No wonder I'd been mated to this stubborn ass. No doubt, very few women could handle him. "That is not your decision to make, Commander Helion. It's mine. And I have thirty days to accept or reject you as my primary male."

"I have made no claim. You should go, find another match."

"You don't have to claim me as yours. The Interstellar Brides' Program has very clear laws. You're mine to accept or reject for the next thirty days, not the other way around." I'd assumed the Prillons wrote their laws that way—giving the female all the power of choice—because they never imagined a warrior who would refuse a matched mate. Until this moment, I'd never imagined it either.

I was not happy to be the first female in Prillon history to be turned away by her perfect match. Ninety-nine percent compatible, they said. Liars. In fact, the shocked look my so-called perfect *mate* gave me, threatened to make me burst into tears.

You are not crying in front of this asshole.

I agreed.

Nothing about this was going the way it was supposed to. In fact, I had planned to be very naked, pressed between two sexy mates, moaning with pleasure as I rode two big cocks by now.

I had plans for a new, secure, and hopefully happy life. I'd be damned if one grumpy Prillon warrior was going to ruin them. Not happening. A centuries old system said he was perfect for me, and I was perfect for him. The moment I signed up to be an Interstellar Bride, I committed to that system with full faith that the matching protocols would deliver the perfect warrior to me. *Commander* Zarren Helion didn't realize that being a monster wouldn't scare me off. Quite the opposite, as long as he was gentle with me.

I wasn't one to wish things were different. No. My time as a captive had taught me how to live moment to moment, deal with the here and now, not worry about a future I couldn't control. I learned quickly. I would adapt and overcome the situation. This strange mate and his odd behavior were nothing more than a puzzle I needed to solve.

Once I had him figured out, I was going to teach this particular Prillon warrior a thing or two about women, specifically *this woman.*

First, I needed to get inside his head. Literally. Where the hell were our mating collars?

"Wait here." I didn't linger to see if he would obey me or not, simply walked into his pathetic excuse for a bedroom and closed the door behind me. I dragged my trunk away from the wall—as promised, it had been waiting when we arrived—just far enough that I could open it. I sank to my knees so I could lift the nearly translucent lingerie from where it lay, carefully folded, on top of the rest of my personal items.

I changed quickly, tugging a bit too hard at the seams of the dress I'd spent hours creating. Zarren didn't seem to like it much. Didn't matter. Moving on. The very first thing every matched warrior, fighter, or beast I'd ever heard of did, once their matched mate arrived, was get naked and get busy. I'd been excited about that part. Really excited.

I'd been shy, when I was younger. Unsure of myself. Scared of feeling shame, instead of pleasure. No more. I'd been naked in a holding cell for months on end. Thank god Nexus 5 never assaulted us while we were awake. He wasn't interested in sex, just science. But walking around in my birthday suit for so long made me very comfortable with my body. In my time recovering on Prillon Prime, I'd learned what I liked and didn't, how to pleasure myself.

When I thought about the Willow who used to live on Earth, I didn't even recognize her. She was like a ghost or a hazy childhood memory.

I slipped the whisper-thin, spaghetti strap, lingerie over my naked flesh and tossed the matching panties back in the trunk. I was going to be fighting an uphill battle here. Didn't need a barrier of any kind between us. And thanks to space-tech and their miracle doctors, I didn't have to worry about birth control, STDs, or even the usual bathroom necessities. As long as I was within range of Coalition transport systems, all my body's natural waste vanished from my insides like magic.

Why would any sane human ever want to go back to Earth?

Feet bare, I strolled over to the S-Gen machine in Zarren's bedroom like I owned the place, which, technically, as the lady of the ship, I did, and put in my order.

"Prillon mating collars, new, set of three." One for me. One for my commander. One for the second I would undoubtedly meet later.

I held my breath as three innocent looking black strips, a bit thicker than ribbon, appeared before my eyes. With a grin, I took one and wrapped it around my neck. As expected, the ribbon adjusted its length to the perfect fit before sinking against my skin and locking itself in place.

Now, all I had to do was get one on my mate and I'd know what the hell was going on in his head. Or at least what he was feeling. As far as I had heard or studied, there was only one mated trio who could actually read one another's minds—thoughts and all—and they started out on The

Colony, their unique psychic link due to the Hive doing some kind of experiments on them.

I only knew about them because one of them was our guardian angel at the sanctuary, my friend Danika. If she could survive what she did to keep her mates, I could deal with this. Right?

I shuddered and pushed Danika, the Hive and the sanctuary out of my head. No more Hive experiments for me, thank you very much. But feeling what Zarren was feeling? Sharing his emotions? I needed that if I was going to keep him. Desperately.

Suddenly unsure, I tucked the third mating collar away inside my trunk before heading for the living room. I didn't know if Zarren would be there when I opened the bedroom door. Didn't have any idea whether he would have stuck around or left me here alone—probably so he could go to his comm station and send some kind of complaint or inquiry as to the Brides' Program's return policy.

Leaning my forehead against the cool door, I counted backward from ten. Slowly. I hid the mating collar, curling it up in the palm of one hand so I could wrap my fingers around it in a tight fist. The collar would bind us together, make our needs and emotions one.

I simply refused to believe Zarren was as cold-hearted and intractable as he seemed. If he were like that on the inside, the matching program would have sent him a robot, not a woman. *Not me.*

Maybe you're more screwed up than you thought? Maybe the program didn't work.

No. I refused to believe that.

Before I could lose my nerve, I opened the door and took two steps into the barren living area. To my relief, Zarren was seated at the table, head bent over his task as he organized his super-secret, not-for-me papers.

Fuck me, he was gorgeous. My nipples tightened into hard pebbles, the soft slide of my nightgown a sensual caress. I wanted his mouth on them, sucking me deep. Or his hands. Hell, I wanted both, everywhere.

My core pulsed, the nearly constant state of arousal I'd been in since the processing simulation roared back to life.

He didn't look at me as I stepped closer, but his nostrils flared. Could he smell my need for him? His hands curled into fists on top of the table. When he spoke, his words were nearly a growl. The tortured sound encouraged me to move even closer.

"What do you think you are doing, female?"

"Claiming my mate."

"I told you, there has been a mistake. You are beautiful, Willow. A beautiful, perfect female. But I did not request a match. This is not right. You cannot be mine. I'm sorry." His voice was soft, a whispered apology I didn't want.

His body remained rigid, his knuckles turning white under his dark skin as I moved to stand directly behind him. Leaning over his shoulder, I placed a soft kiss on the side of his neck, pulled the scent of him into my lungs. His essence didn't stop there. No, it jumped into my bloodstream and made a beeline for my pussy. My knees went weak and I barely held back a very needy moan. "Are you sure you don't want me?"

God help me, I wanted him. Even my inner voice remained quiet, waiting.

"I didn't say—you are lovely. I can't—" He did growl this time, dropping his chin to his chest. "I am trying to protect you. There is no place in my life for a female. I will hurt you, Willow. I will break your heart—"

"Perhaps." So, he *did* want me, at least physically. Trying to protect me? From what? Himself? No. I've survived living hell. He was my shield against monsters in the real world, not the evil that haunted my nightmares.

"Willow, I won't love you. Do you understand? I can fuck you and provide for you, but I won't love you. I will never love you the way you deserve to be loved."

He sounded like he actually believed what he was saying. "Why not?"

I watched as a shudder moved through him, head to toe. His next words startled me, like he'd slipped an ice cube inside my shirt. "Because if I loved you, I would always choose you. I would let thousands die to save you, sacrifice innocent lives for my selfish need to protect you. Do you understand?"

I did. Completely. And the guilt he carried? Perhaps he had made one of those selfish decisions, had loved someone, and that someone had died as a result. That story, that darkness, was his burden to carry. I would not ask him to set it aside. His current choice was honorable, duty before self. Service to the many, rather than the one. It was admirable, really. Made me even more convinced he was the right mate for me. That processing computer really did know its stuff.

Right now I needed to make him understand that he was exactly what I needed.

"I understand." I moved directly behind him, pressed my body to his, melted against him, let his heat, the leashed power inside him, sink into my body. God, it felt good. I hadn't felt this calm since—since before. I wasn't giving this up without a fight. Love was fragile and fleeting. A daydream. Fantasy, not reality. "So don't love me, commander. I don't need you to love me. I just need you to keep me close and make me feel safe."

I slipped my hands around his neck until my fingers met. Zarren's chin lifted and he leaned back to rest his head against my body. I took one end of the mating collar in each hand and moved my arms back, like I was putting a necklace on him, my skin lightly grazing his. I kissed the top of his head. "I know you don't believe me, so feel me."

Zarren lifted a hand to his neck. He traced the line of the collar I held, his fingertips moving up and around until his hand covered mine, holding me in place, preventing the final connection. "You aren't going to like what you find, if you place that collar around my neck."

"What is it you think I'm going to discover?"

"A heart and mind that will never be able to love you." His hand squeezed mine to emphasize his words. "I do not jest, Willow Baylor. Duty will always be first for me. I neither want, nor need, emotional distraction."

"I believe you." I leaned over and rested my cheek on top of his head. "I need you to believe me. Love is not necessary, mate. Pleasure and protection, that is all I will ever ask of you. Once we are comfortable together, I will request that you choose a second. Your activity in the war is not without risk, and I don't want to be left alone if something were to happen to you."

"That is a reasonable request. No male of worth would leave you to survive alone."

Relieved he was listening—finally—and not arguing with me, I pressed on. "In return, I will by loyal to you, only you, and provide you with comfort and company." I sighed as I looked at the empty room all around me. "We can be friends, Zarren. On Earth, we would call this a marriage of convenience. Two people choosing a partner for the external benefits each will receive, rather than emotional dependence. But I must warn you, there will be furniture in this room when I am your mate. And a bigger bed."

"And children? Most females want that. I will not father children while the war continues."

I sighed, partially with sadness. Mostly in relief. The idea of being responsible for the care and safety of a completely helpless infant terrified me. The universe was too dangerous and violent for little ones. "I do not need children to be content."

His quickly drawn breath revealed his unease. "I do not understand you, female."

"You don't have to make sense of it, you just need to believe what I say is true."

He shuddered. "I am a monster, Willow. Nothing less."

I smiled. "Then you are exactly what I need." A monster so big, mean and scary that all the other monsters—and Nexus units—would run away and hide—and leave me the hell alone. With my commander, I would be safe, hidden away on his spaceship, surrounded by warriors—but no longer lonely.

I'd never felt more sure, more calm, about a decision in my life.

This is a mistake, woman. You won't be happy.

Shut up. Yes, I will.

I could practically feel a part of me shaking her head in disapproval. So? So what if this wasn't the relationship I had dreamed about when I was ten years old and imagining my future husband. One, I didn't even know aliens existed back then. And two—Zarren was hot. Strong. Honorable. He said this was his ship, so he wasn't dirt poor. What else did a woman need?

His hand shifted, moved the end of the collar we held to

meet its opposite at the back of his neck. The mating collar locked in place.

A hurricane of raw lust blasted my system. I gasped at the force of Zarren's emotions, unable to hide my shock at the ferocity. So outwardly calm. Stoic. Controlled.

Inside? A storm. Battle. He hurt. He raged. He *wanted.*

7

Willow

Holy shit. Now that the collars were synched, his emotions roared around inside me like hurricane force winds. I took them all, savored his desire, raw need, and a deep, powerful rage I had never allowed myself to feel.

He shot to his feet, the back of the chair he had been sitting in knocked into me before teetering and falling on its side. "What have we done?"

Relief flooded me, second only to desire. "I told you, Commander, I am not a love-sick fool. I am the perfect mate for you, as you are for me." I stared at his back, my gaze tracing the shifting muscle under his uniform, his broad shoulders, trim waist. God, I wanted to bite his ass, not too hard, just a nibble really. It was so tight and perfect. I stepped back and looked up at the black silk of his hair, longed to run my fingers through it, kiss his neck, his cheek. His lips. Breathe him in. Be with him.

"Fuck. This is insane." His breath had become ragged and unsteady.

His words made my pussy clench. He thought he was being honorable? Protecting me? From what? I was in his head now, at least in his emotions. He had not lied to me, I sensed no love, just loneliness and resignation. He had made his choices, as I made mine.

I wasn't afraid. The opposite, in fact. He was perfect. It wouldn't matter to him that I was broken inside, that I was anxious all the time. Because with him as my mate, I wouldn't be. Not anymore. With him, I could let my body relax and just be—satisfied.

I wanted to climb him, strip him, ride him until we both passed out. I rubbed at my swollen nipples with both hands, imagined the touch came from him. Imagined what it would feel like to be stuffed full of his cock, sliding up and down his hard length—

"Gods, female, you have lost your fucking mind." His shock was real. I felt it through our connection, the communication between our mating collars was strong. Really damn strong. "If you don't stop that, I'm going to lose control."

"Turn around, Zarren."

"No."

"But I'm wearing your gift."

A stab of curiosity and...surprise? He shoved both emotions down at once.

If he didn't accept me, he would not allow another match to happen, he would take no bride. I was sure of it. Just as sure that he meant what he said. He didn't want to care so much about one person that he would sacrifice countless others on their behalf.

The choice was honorable. Admirable. And so damn lonely my heart ached for him. Without me, he would bury his soul in duty, seek no comfort. Might as well get that doctor in here and ask him to cut Zarren's heart from his chest. It would be a blessing for him, not to carry so much pain, such unbearable guilt.

"You must keep your word. I would turn you away, rather than fail to provide what you need to be happy. I cannot live with another failure. I would never forgive myself if I broke your heart."

"I promise you, I will never ask you to love me. Never expect you to change. But I won't change either. I will admire and respect you, as I already do. I will feel desire and enjoy sex, but that is all." I couldn't fall in love, my heart was too fragmented to accomplish such a feat. "I promise."

I meant every word. No use lying to one another when the collars would give us away. Better to understand one another from the beginning.

I would think of this as an adventure. I would play the part of a royal princess married to a stranger, a powerful king with a massive army at his command. An arrangement between two kingdoms rather than a love match. I was like Juliet, except the dream of a perfect Romeo was already dead, and I already had the dagger through my heart.

A pit of emptiness welled up inside me. Not just his, mine. Years of captivity. Months of wandering aimlessly through the sanctuary on Prillon Prime, avoiding contact with another living soul. Other than an occasional hug from Makayla, I'd gone months without physical touch.

Maybe he wouldn't love me, but he could touch me, make me feel like a real woman rather than a puppet made of wood.

Let me out. Stop pretending.

No.

I shoved the memories, the darkness, aside—as I always did—and focused my complete attention on now. Right now. Zarren's strong body so close I could feel his heat, our shared attraction, longing for touch, for connection. The need came from a deep, dark well I had learned to ignore. Except, he had one, too.

Unable to resist for another moment, I lifted my hand and placed my palm flat on his back. "I promise. Please don't send me away. I need this."

My vow was like lightning in his body. Anticipation warred with need as he pulled his shirt off over his head. He turned around, his green eyes inspecting every detail of my sheer nightie—it wasn't long, the hem at mid-thigh—before inspecting my legs and lower, down to my bright silver toenails. On the way back up, his attention lingered on the vee between my legs, on the firm nipples beckoning him through the shimmering fabric. He reached out with one hand and lifted a strand of my hair, watched it fall like liquid gold through his fingers.

"I made this for you. Well, I didn't know you were going to be you, but I made it for my first night with my—"

His lips pressed to mine before I could finish the sentence. *My mate. My first night with my mate.*

One taste and we both lost our minds—or mind? I couldn't distinguish his need from mine. His lust. His desire. I wanted his hands everywhere, as he wanted mine. I fumbled at his clothing until he took over, uncaring where anything ended up. The moment he was naked, I reached for his huge cock, wrapped two hands around its girth and stroked him the way his body told me he liked it. Firm. Fast.

We both moaned as I cupped his balls and pulled his

nipple into my mouth. Jolts of pleasure shot from every place our bodies touched, straight to my throbbing cock. Shit—*his* cock. His senses were drifting, combining with mine.

God, these collars were going to turn me into a sex-crazed maniac.

I whimpered and rubbed my breasts against him. They were heavy. Achy and super sensitive. My pussy was hot, wet and starving for attention. Fuck that, for a big cock to stretch me open and make me come, make me shudder as my inner muscles fluttered and squeezed him, pulled him deeper, milked him dry. I wanted to lock my legs over his hips and hang on for dear life as he pressed my back to the wall and fucked me. Hard. Fast.

I wanted him buried balls deep, my hot, tight pussy like an inferno burning my sensitive skin—wait, that was his skin...

Was that what it felt like to slide his cock inside a woman's body?

Fuuuck. I—he—could smell my wetness, my empty, aching need, and it was driving him mad. Literally, beyond thought, to where instinct alone ruled his body.

I wanted him wild. I prayed his body would need mine as much as I needed his. I was so hungry for touch, for contact. Connection. I'd been alone—so damn alone for so long in that cell...

"No. Not alone." His gruff words broke me free as he lifted me off the floor and carried me to the wall. He held me there, pinned and unable—unwilling—to break free. His mouth claimed mine, every emotion coming from him possessive. Protective.

The psychic link between us hit me like a truckload of bricks. I was safe. He was a killer, and no one would ever get near me, ever hurt me—hell, ever scare me again. Ever. I soaked him in, clinging to that knowledge, to the belonging I craved as I wrapped my fingers around his dark hair and held his lips to mine. Devoured him.

He moved one hand down to the curve of my bottom until he could tease the soft lips of my core with his fingertips.

One of his fingers slipped inside my body, traced the soft, throbbing edges, pulled my pussy open just enough to—

He pushed two fingers deep. Fucked me with firm, powerful strokes. Filled me. Pushed me over the hard edge I'd been riding.

I tore my lips from his. My head fell back as my loud cry echoed through the room. His fingers pumped in and out of my body as the orgasm rolled through me.

He played, his touch guided—no doubt—by the wild pleasure building inside me.

I was close to coming again. I hadn't come down from the ledge. So close.

His hand fell away. I cried out in protest and locked my hands onto his shoulders, trying to pull him closer.

He shifted. His lust mingled with mine. He pushed his cock deep in one long, slow thrust.

My pussy opened, pulled him in and closed around him. So wet. So tight, like a vice made of sunlight, almost burning him alive.

The sensations—his—filled my mind as my own body became nothing and everything all at once. There was nothing but his heat pressed to my chest, his hands on my ass, my lips moving frantically over his skin, his taste exploding on my tongue.

And his cock. God. His cock was huge. Hard. I was full, stretched to the limit.

I needed him to move. I was unable. My feet were behind his back, my body pinned to the wall by the hard length deep inside me. So deep. So good. I whimpered. Why was he holding back when I knew he could feel what I felt, when he knew what I liked, what I wanted.

He held me in place, unmoving, the pressure inside me building, clawing its way through my blood to my core. If he didn't finish this, pound his hips against mine and fuck me, I was going to lose it. Beg. Fucking beg.

I couldn't force him to move. I was powerless, at his mercy, and so turned on I had to fight to hold back a sob, to keep myself from pleading, exposing my weakness, as his lust and mine spiraled together.

This was insane. I never wanted it to end, and I would literally go mad if it didn't.

Please, please move.

Zarren Helion

I should have run the moment I saw her curves through the transparent fabric. Her breasts were too close, the nipples tight, inviting me to taste. The exposed skin of her legs, from mid-thigh to her delicate, adorable feet, looked softer than I could have imagined. She'd brought the seductive clothing for me, not realizing she wouldn't be *wearing* my 'gift'. She was the gift.

She'd planned to wear the short, ethereal gown for her *mate*. I had a mate, a female who vowed not to love me and expected no love in return. A *marriage of convenience,* she'd said. A normal arrangement on Earth? Maybe, if I repeated the words enough times, I could live with them.

I was fucked.

Literally, her eager pussy had swallowed my cock. Now the hot, wet heat of her wrapped me up so tight I couldn't move. Didn't want to move. Ever. For the rest of my fucking life.

She was wild, unlike anything I'd ever imagined a female could be. Her eager lips moved over my chest like I was the best thing she'd ever tasted. I was. Her raw desire coated my mind like a pitcher of hot water poured over ice.

Like ice, I felt myself cracking. Breaking. Losing strength and integrity every moment I spent submerged.

Her small body cost me no effort to hold in place against the wall. I held her steady, gently, as I wrestled control from a feral side of myself, a side I'd hoped to never see again.

One fucking day—less, a few hours in her presence—and the monster was back, stronger than before. He was my own personal beast. I wasn't Atlan. I didn't transform, but what I had buried deep was worse, a colossal nightmare. Selfish. Insidious. Utterly and completely single-minded. War meant nothing. Death meant nothing. He didn't waste time with guilt or remorse. There was but one calculation he would accept, the sums calculated with stark, brutal efficiency. For seven years I'd kept his attention focused on winning the war.

She'd turned his head. His new sum, focus and obsession?

Her. Fucking her. Keeping her close. Safe.

I gritted my teeth and fought for control as her pussy clenched and released. Willow squeezed me again, her soft moan pure fire in my blood. I wanted to hear her make that sound again. And again.

She shifted—as much as she was able—her hips moving just enough to slide her pussy up, then down, around the very base of my cock. She couldn't move much, couldn't escape. Couldn't come until I gave her that pleasure. She was mine, completely at my mercy, my body buried deep inside hers.

If I'd sensed fear or remorse from her, I could have walked away. Regret. Trepidation. Worry. Anything but surrender, total and complete trust. Pleasure. Acceptance. She was exactly where she wanted to be, riding my cock, licking and kissing me, waiting—impatiently—for me to thrust in and out, take her on a ride, make her pussy melt all over my cock as I pushed her to another orgasm.

And another.

The need to do so, to give her exactly what her body needed, clawed at my already shattered conscience. She needed. It was as simple—and complicated—as that.

"Willow." Her name was both prayer and curse leaving my lips. She never should have made that vow. She should have walked away. Too fucking late now. She gave me her word and she'd meant it. Promised me it would be safe to take what she offered. Sex without strings, two adults who agreed to give and receive pleasure. Comfort. Another being with whom I could allow myself to be touched, to hold someone. To pretend I could live a normal life and know I wasn't going to hurt her or break her heart with my complete focus on duty? On protecting my people?

That demon inside me snarled a warning. He wanted to pound in and out of Willow's body, fill her with seed and then lower her to the hard floor and do it all again.

She'd asked for a second. I tried to imagine what it would be like to share her with another, hold her between us as we both fucked her. Watch another male touch her.

Comfort her. Hold her in his arms as she slept—vulnerable and unaware.

The monster howled. He didn't want to share.

I shoved him back in his mental cage and drew the scent of my mate deep into my lungs. I would focus now, on what I *could* give her.

Pleasure.

8

Zarren Helion

THE FLOOR WOULD BE TOO hard for her, she would bruise. The bed. I'd carry her there, bend her over the edge and take her from behind. Gods, her ass would look spectacular as I pulled her flush to my hips. Filled her up. Made her squirm.

"Zarren, move!" Willow's words were followed by her soft whimper. "Please, please, move."

I felt her let go of whatever piece of herself she'd been holding back. She relinquished her body, her need. Everything. I was there, in her head. She would stay with me, live with me, give me her body, and ask for nothing but protection in return. Stay with the monster who had destroyed worlds to save one life. And failed.

Terror hovered at the edge of my consciousness, but I shoved it back, locked it away so Willow would not feel it through our link.

I lifted her body, slid her pussy to the very tip of my cock, and lowered her again. She groaned, her entire being balanced on the edge of another release. She weighed nothing, so I lifted and lowered her again. And again. Her sighs became mine, the stimulation—her pussy stretched by my cock—my cock surrounded by tight, hot ridges—flowed between us like water sloshing from side to side in a pitcher. Her pleasure. Mine.

Emptiness. Disappointment.

"Willow? What is it?"

"Don't stop."

I leaned forward, pressing her into the wall, and pushed deep, lifting her with the strength of my thrusting cock. "Tell me what you need."

She sighed. Squirmed. Realized I was resolute.

"It's just, there were supposed to be two of you..." Her voice trailed off. Of course, Prillon warriors always mated in pairs, fucked their female together when they claimed her.

Did she ache for a second cock, filling her from behind, making her feel safe between two? Chosen by two? Never abandoned or left to fend for herself? I was not enough.

"Fuck."

"It's okay. Just keep going. Don't stop. I'll kill you if you stop now." Willow's threats were meant to appease me, assuage my guilt. I had no second, had never chosen a male to curse with my solitary existence.

I could not solve that problem at the moment, but I could assist with another.

Moving with purpose, I fucked her, thrust deep. Pulled out. Three times. Four.

She moaned.

Cock buried to the hilt, I stopped and reached around to access the device implanted in every Prillon bride's gorgeous, perfect ass. The devices used to prepare a mate to accept both warriors' cocks at the same time had been primitive until recently. Hard, externally placed objects that required time, care, and external lubrication. But this?

I teased her with a slight movement of one finger near her second opening. She had the newest upgrade implanted there, as all brides received during their processing. Now that we wore mating collars, I could use my implanted comm device to adjust the settings, turn it on and off. Release lubrication. Make the implant larger, make it vibrate or send small shocks through her nerves, directly to her clit.

"What?" Willow's surprise devolved into a loud moan as the device grew to fill her ass. I stopped the expansion when I could feel the pressure from within her pussy as the implant filled her and pushed against my cock. "Oh, god."

"Is this what you need?"

"Yes."

One quick thrust of my cock and she came apart in my arms. I fucked her and filled her, made her come twice more before I gave in, let my cock have its way, moving faster and harder, quick shallow movements. Deep strokes. I lost the rhythm, my body taking over in an uncontrollable frenzy.

Willow cried out, her pussy shifting into spasms, her orgasm pushing me over the edge. I kept pumping my hips, mindlessly pushing my seed deeper and deeper, needing to mark her. Claim her. Fill her.

When it was over, I deactivated the anal device and pulled her against my chest. She melted against me, accepting. Trusting. Cock still inside her, I carried her to the bathing room and stepped under the warm spray. Her barely there clothing was soaked instantly, the material clung, hiding nothing.

I washed her, the action an excuse to continue touching her, exploring every curve. My cock, bastard that he was, stayed hard and refused to leave her body. The demanding monster within refused to separate my body from hers. She languished in my arms, her smile soft and dreamy as I held her in place but didn't protest.

By the time I finished, my cock throbbed, ached to take her again. By the gods, she was too fucking beautiful.

I settled my back against the wall and, still holding her in place, slid down into a seated position so Willow's back remained under the flow of warm water—I wouldn't allow her to be cold. Her skin was slippery, and her thighs glided down along my sides as I shifted her hips, her hot pussy settled in place over my hard length. She took me deeper, her swollen center still very, very wet, and ready. Greedy.

"You are so naughty." The laughter in her voice made me smile. The expression felt unnatural, like a lie perched on my face.

"I am." Moving slowly, I spread my hands across her back and arched her chest up toward my mouth. I had yet to taste her nipples and the need was riding me. Hard. I locked my lips around one wet peak and pulled the flesh into my mouth. Wet fabric kept her softness from me.

With a snarl, I grabbed the garment and lifted it completely off, over her head, and tossed it aside. "I'm going to fuck you again."

Willow arched her back, offering her body for my tasting. Her eyes were closed so I couldn't see her expression. Her lips and cheeks were relaxed. She looked innocent and untouched, sleepy. Not aroused or in need.

The only thing coming through the collars was... confusing. Satisfaction and desire. Urgency and exhaustion. Pleasure as well as discomfort, a throbbing ache everywhere her pussy stretched around my cock.

"Do you want me to stop? Are you in pain?" Had I hurt her? Fucked her too hard? Held her too tightly? Kept our bodies connected too long?

"No. And no." Hearing her contented sigh, I relaxed as she lifted her arms to wrap them around my head, rubbed her breast against my lips. As if to emphasize her words, her inner muscles squeezed me, the resulting jolt of pleasure from both of us mingling through our connection. "I like naughty."

Fuck me, so did I.

Willow, Three Nights Later

I always knew when I was sleeping when what I saw was only nightmarish. Not real. Something Nexus 5 had done to me during one of his experiments had changed the way I dreamed.

I didn't live my dreams or participate in them like I used to. Since my captivity, I watched everything happen, like watching a movie, except I could feel what was happening to the main character on screen—always me—another version of me.

Me—watching me—*feeling* what movie screen me was going through.

'Cuz two of us in my head wasn't enough.

Me—and old me—both chuckled at the absurdity of the thought.

I'd never asked the other escapees if they experienced the same duality of mind. Seemed too personal of a question. Everyone argued with themselves. I'd done it before, back on Earth. It just felt like more of a real conversation now. Over time, I'd concluded that monitoring my mind as I slept was just another facet of Nexus 5's experiments. Whatever he'd done had changed the way my mind operated. Asleep. Awake. I was different. I could compartmentalize in a way I never could before, literally, put pain-in-the-ass me into a mental box and lock her ass down.

Don't you dare.

Then be quiet, we're dreaming.

I know.

I stood outside my old prison cell in his lab and watched another version of myself—movie screen me—curl into a ball on a firm sleeping pad and shiver uncontrollably. Teeth chattering. Toes aching from the cold, beginning the process of going numb.

Our captor kept the rooms cold when he didn't want us to sleep. Sometimes for days. I shivered as I watched dream me run her hands over her arms in an attempt to warm them. Felt the chilled skin under my own palms, the hunger gnawing at her also a cavernous ache in my observer's body.

Then I saw *him*. Dark blue skin, black uniform, eyes black and dull as matte paint dried on weathered wood. Prison me looked up at him and glared, still defiant. Still fighting.

"Why are you doing this?" she demanded.

His answer appeared; words pushed into my mind. *I must determine the limits of your system's tolerance to environmental living conditions.*

"Why?"

I do not wish to limit human reproductive capabilities by exposing your bodies to extremes beyond which your species can adapt. Our males can live in extreme environments. Human females are much more fragile. A successful, native breeding program will require ideal conditions be maintained for our female subjects.

Reproductive capabilities? Breeding program? Horror at his words spiraled inside me—both of me—with all the panic and revulsion I'd felt the *first* time I'd experienced this moment, realized what my new captor intended. Why we were all here. I was not the only woman who had been captured and sold to this—*thing.*

"I will kill myself before I let you do that to me." Primal rage rose inside me, even more powerful than my terror. I would not carry this creature's child, let it live and grow inside me like a parasite. A disgusting, alien parasite.

Successful gestation has already begun.

No!

I would starve myself to death. Claw out my own throat. I would—

Unfortunate. Your lack of cooperation is illogical.

Dream me opened her mouth to scream her rage, but no sound emerged. With one look, Nexus 5 had taken control of her—my body. He issued an order, instantly obeyed.

Sleep.

I WOKE WITH A GASP, which I immediately silenced. I didn't want to bother Zarren, and I didn't want to answer any questions. I knew how to stay still, shut down the panic, and wait.

You're welcome.

Yes, there was a reason I didn't truly shut down that part of myself. I needed her. She was the only reason I'd survived.

Our bedroom was dark, the only light from a slender band next to the door that glowed a soft blue. The commander had wanted the room to be pitch black, *'in the event we were boarded'*. I'd simply told him I needed enough light to find my way out or I wouldn't be sleeping with him.

My nightlight had been installed within hours.

I'd accomplished a lot in the last few days, once I'd found the location of their cargo hold, where the largest S-Gen machines were usually found.

We had a new, much larger bed—I'd kept the black sheets. I was either having wild sex, or asleep when I was in bed, and they made my commander content. We probably didn't even need the larger bed. He slept with me wrapped snuggly, securely in his arms, my entire body pressed against him. We didn't take up a lot of room. But he had promised me a second, when I was ready. We would definitely need a bigger bed when there were three of us. And there would be three. I hadn't changed my mind about that, and neither had he. The question now was who he would trust with caring for me. A decision he said he did not wish to rush.

I believed him, but I also knew finding a warrior he could live with was an equally delicate task.

Pulse slowed to a reasonable pounding, rather than the explosive speed of a hummingbird's, I stole out from the arm wrapped around my waist and tip-toed to the door. I'd placed two hooks on the wall and matching robes hung from each. I slipped my arms into the soft sleeves of the smaller garment and tied the belt around my waist as I walked into our newly furnished living room.

The bedroom door closed behind me without making a sound. I stood still, listening for my commander. When I heard nothing to indicate he was awake, I sighed in relief.

You're going to have to tell him everything.

Not yet. I wasn't ready to talk about any of it.

You can't keep this up.

I ignored her.

"Lamp on, low." I whispered the order and the ship responded, activating the soft glow of a delicately carved table lamp I'd designed with the S-Gen machine. The shiny surface was a soft rose color, the flowing form meant to trick the eye as the outline of a woman melted into that of a swan —and back again, if one circled the lamp. The matching sofas, one large, one perfect for two, were a gentle, soft gray decorated with pale pink and darker gray pillows and soft blankets. The temperature of the room was controlled at all times, but he would adjust the settings for my comfort, my mate informed me, pleased with himself. I explained to him the plush cushions and cozy blankets were for comfort, not necessity. Comfort—he'd looked around the room but said nothing. I thought he'd dismissed my comment, and my need. I was wrong. So wrong.

To his credit, he'd adapted quickly, insisting on bending me over the back of the couch and making me melt all over his cock—a soft pillow under my hips to ensure my '*comfort*'. Even now, the memory made me blush. By the end of the next night, Zarren had used the S-Gen machine to create multiple items 'for my comfort', including two lengths of soft fabric he'd used, one to blindfold me, the other to tie my hands over my head while he made me come.

I'd unpacked my suitcase, placing the few items I'd brought with me into a drawer built into the wall of the bedroom. I was making this a home, as much as I could in just a few days. I'd activated the entertainment settings on the large comm screen—Zarren only ever used it for official Intelligence Core or military business—so I could watch literally anything I wanted while he was working, from human sitcoms to educational vids on ship engineering, or detailed documentaries about various planets in the Coalition.

I should be content, at peace. *Happy.* I had never felt safer or more secure, more certain about my future.

But the nightmares were killing me. They bubbled up from my subconscious and forced their way into my dreams, cut spaces in my mind like glaciers carving valleys. Even after they were gone, the scarred landscape remained.

Reaching into the robe's pocket, I lifted my mating collar from its hiding place and secured it around my neck. I held myself still as the connection linked me to my sleeping mate. Calm. Silent. Empty. I did not want to send any strong emotions that might wake him.

After the first night, I'd learned to remove the collar when I slept. I would wait, make my mind calm and clear, focus on the contentment coming from my commander until he drifted off to sleep, and then take my collar off.

There was no need for him to suffer with me every night, and I did not wish to answer any questions.

Nightmares were just dreams in darkness. I did not intend to breathe life into them in the light of day. Well, spaceship day. There wasn't exactly a star that rose and set on the horizon. Luckily, all the ships set their schedules to match the capital city's time on Prillon Prime. Their planet's natural length of day was close enough to Earth's that adjusting my body's circadian rhythm had been easy.

I glanced at the data pad embedded in the wall near the front door. As I suspected, it was nearly morning. Zarren would wake on his own soon, as would the rest of the warriors on the ship. Wake, work, eat...

Fuck.

Naked under the robe, I was suddenly acutely aware of everywhere the fabric moved over my skin, flowed around my things and ass, hugged my breasts.

I settled my palms along the back of the couch where, not long ago, my commander had bent me over and filled me with his cock. Thrust deep. Pulled my back to his chest and cupped my breasts from behind.

"By the gods, female, you have a one track mind." Big, strong hands slipped around my waist, reaching for the tie securing my robe.

9

Zarren Helion

SHE SHIVERED, but not from cold. Was she responding to my touch? Or still upset about whatever nightmare had driven her from my arms this morning? Every morning since her arrival. I fought myself, told myself it was none of my business. Me. The one male in the universe who, as far as I was aware, had more knowledge about what was happening than any other.

Yet I knew nothing about my own mate.

I slid my hands around her and pulled her small body back, against mine. "Tell me why you remove your mating collar at night."

"It's nothing. I don't want to talk about it." She shifted her weight, turning to face me. I wasn't sure if her intent was to get away from me, or to move closer. When she pressed her lips to my chest, I assumed it was the latter.

"Are you trying to distract me, female?"

"Would I do that?" She kissed me again, then moved to take one nipple into her small mouth. Delicate hands reached between us and grabbed my cock, wrapped around me and squeezed just hard enough to make me moan.

Fuck me, this female was dangerous. "Yes. You would." I knew that much.

I lifted my hands to cup each side of her jaw and angled her face until she looked at me, her gaze locked with mine, her fists locked around my throbbing cock. "I am an intelligence officer, commander of the I.C. I wouldn't be very good at my job if I didn't notice what has happening with my own mate."

Something dark and fleeting flashed through her eyes, something I'd never seen before. Before I could ask more questions, Willow sank to her knees on the thick rug that now covered most of the room and sucked my hard length into her mouth. Her tongue teased the underside with an insistent flicker that drove sane thought from my head.

"Damn it, female." My cock swelled, became painfully engorged in seconds.

She pulled back, held my cock in place with her hands and rubbed her lips back and forth across the tip. "Do you want me to stop?"

"No." Fuck no.

She sucked me deep. I nearly lost my balance. This was new, something she had never done before. I snarled and brought my hands down on the back of our new sofa to brace myself. I'd spent more than a little time seated here, holding Willow as she watched one of her strange entertainment vids and laughed. She was allowed to watch until I couldn't resist touching her, trying to share her happiness, rub some of her joy onto myself.

She increased her pace and moved one of her hands to

tease my balls. Fire gathered in my blood; the heat concentrated everywhere she touched me. Licked me. Sucked like she was trying to pull the seed from my balls. Gods, she was fucking relentless. I wouldn't last long.

"Enough. I will fuck you now." Yes. That's what I would do. Lift her off the floor, bend her over the couch and push my hard cock into her wet heat, pump into her until she cried out, make her forget everything until there was only me. Only. Me. A fucking dangerous thing to want, but I couldn't stop the thought from pounding inside my skull like a drum. No one else would fuck her. Kiss her. Touch her. Hold her. No one. Only me.

I assumed she would obey my command and release me. Instead, she looked up at me, hands firmly wrapped around me, and shook her head. "No. I'm still sore, I haven't used a ReGen wand yet, and besides—I want to do this. Just relax, Zarren. Feel my touch. Let me make you come."

What the fu—

She sucked my cock until it bumped the back of her throat and ran her fingernails down my thighs. Before I could recover, she reached behind me, did the same to my sensitive ass.

She worked some kind of sorcery on me because I couldn't move, couldn't do anything but stand still and tremble as she staked her claim. She wouldn't do this for any other male. Only me. Because she was mine.

I was hers. She fucking owned me. Perfect. Hot. Wet. Mate...

My orgasm hit without warning, hard and fast and so fucking strong I was shaking when she finished with me. She swallowed me down with ferocious greed, her desire to please me clear as a bell ringing through our linked collars. She wanted me like this, under her spell, giving her control and allowing her to take whatever she wanted. It wasn't just her desire; it was a *need*. Desperation. Distraction.

What the fuck was going on here?

I reached down and lifted her into my arms, cradling her to my chest. I held her close and curled my body over and around hers, buried my face just beneath her ear. Kissed her neck. She melted against me, as I had come to expect. And crave.

Tonight, she would tell me what bothered her. If I had time now, I would not relent, but duty called. First and foremost, I would serve the Coalition. I could not put off my meeting not knowing what knowledge or advantage I would gain.

"I have to leave you for a few hours." I had to go to Transport Station Zenith, a space station near this sector that was well known as a dangerous place, despite being under the Coalition's control. One of my operatives on Rogue 5 had sent a meeting request. Recruiting one of those fanged bastards was nearly impossible, so I answered when they called—which wasn't often.

Perhaps he had discovered some information about my prisoner and the Hive base. Mersan had spent the last three days working on the Arcas bastard, and he still hadn't given us a single, useful word.

All I had to go on was ink on paper. I spent hours poring over the schematics, looking for a clue, any hint as to where the Hive base had been built. Willow had insisted we put the drawings away when I wasn't looking at them. A break from work, she'd said.

As I generally spent my time holding her, or fucking her, I hadn't complained.

"Okay. Can you ask one of your guys to come take me to

lunch? I'd like to get out of here for a while today. I'm starting to feel cooped up."

"Of course." Warlord Razmus or Elite Hunter Kayn were the only two I'd trusted with her safety to this point. I was sure one, or both, would be pleased to have an excuse to do something other than work. I breathed her in, lingering for another stolen moment. She wasn't heavy. I could stand right here, holding her like this, for hours. "But when I get back, we are going to discuss your habit of removing your mating collar."

"I'll think about it." She wiggled and pushed against my shoulders. With a shocking amount of reluctance, I set her on her feet, picked up her fallen robe and then wrapped her up in it so she wouldn't get cold. She turned her face away from me, kept her gave averted.

This wasn't a love match; her pouting should have no effect on me. So why did I want to pull the hair from my head and throw things, violently, around the room? This was a communication issue, nothing more. One that would be dealt with. Tonight.

I scolded her as I retied the ribbon that held the fabric closed, hiding her beautiful, perfectly curved body from me so I wouldn't be quite as tempted.

"You are mine. It is my duty to care for you. I cannot do that if you are keeping secrets." Even though I did not love her, I was her mate in every way that mattered. It was my responsibility to ensure she was properly taken care of.

"That's rich, don't you think, coming from the king of secrets?"

So sassy. I wanted to kiss that sass right out of her mouth. "My work for the Coalition does not affect what happens between us." Cold, hard logic could never be argued against.

With a shrug, she walked toward the bedroom. "I'm going to take a shower. We can argue about this when you get home."

Home. For fucks sake, I had one now. This barren dungeon in which I had imprisoned myself had become a place of comfort, solace, and pleasure. Thanks to the female who was now out of sight.

Argue? There would be no argument. She would tell me what I needed to know, or I would put my mouth to work teasing her pussy. Two could play this game. I would devour her, but not allow her to come, until she told me *everything*.

Willow

I grinned in silence as Kayn escorted me to the small eating area on board the ship. It wasn't a cafeteria, more like a big dining room with one table and fourteen chairs.

My blow job assault had worked its magic and shut Zarren up. I'd used his pleasure—coming like wildfire through the mating collars—to distract myself from the truth. I didn't want to think about it, but he was going to make me discuss it with him when he got home. Tonight. I wouldn't be able to lie to him—or myself—any longer.

I wasn't okay. In fact, I was so damn far from okay, I didn't recognize myself.

Thank god. It's about time. Now we can talk...

No. I'm not ready for you yet.

Pink and gray? I hated both colors, like seriously hated them since elementary school. I preferred bright reds, vibrant blues, and greens. Sunflower yellow. Colors that were full of energy and caught the eye. Orange. God, I loved bright orange.

So why had I turned our quarters into a sad, under stimulating, completely without personality, hiding place?

Because I felt safe there. That's why. Unobtrusive. Hushed. Soft and unremarkable in every way. The room didn't make me feel anything at all except quiet. The male who kept me company there? He was the polar opposite of boring. Zarren was fabulous. Sexy. Strong. Scary. Attentive. He hadn't said he loved me, but that was the agreement. The real question? Was I falling in love with him?

He feels good.

I knew what she meant. When I was connected to him, I felt what he felt—and not just during sex. Every moment we were together. He was confident. Strong.

Fearless.

Was I falling in love with Zarren, or with the way he made me feel? Did it matter?

I sighed. I had plenty of time to figure all that out later. Right now, I was hungry.

I'd veered from my norm and settled on a soft pair of leggings and matching tunic with stomp-around boots, rather than a dress and slippers. The outfit was lined and very warm because the ship tended to be cold. I didn't care what my mate said about the temperature being controlled, it was cold. Outer space was frigid. It was like the abyss outside the ship's hull sent cold thoughts inside.

Or maybe it was the constant threat of instant annihilation. One little thing goes wrong and...poof. We'd all be dead.

Space sucked.

"My lady, please, sit anywhere you'd like." Elite Hunter Kayn indicated the large table with a sweep of one arm as he walked to the S-Gen machine. "What can I order for you?"

"Chicken Parmigiana, please. With extra spaghetti, a piece of garlic bread and a glass of Merlot." I could drink with lunch, right? It was five o'clock somewhere. Probably multiple somewheres. Since I seemed to be having trouble taking a deep breath—anxiety is a mother fucker—I needed to relax, at least a little. I rarely drank, so the wine would help me nap until Zarren was finished working.

"Of course."

I didn't expect him to remember my order, but he repeated it verbatim. Only one seat at the table was occupied. The doctor I'd seen my first day on the ship appeared to have finished eating and was twirling a half-empty glass of dark red liquid in one hand. He stared into the liquid like it held the answers to every mystery in the universe.

I'll take a glass of what he's having, please.

"May I?" I stood directly across the table from him.

The doctor looked up at me. "Of course, my lady."

I sat as Kayn placed my perfectly prepared meal before me. The doctor looked at my wine. "Is that a wine from Earth?"

"It is."

He looked at Kayn. "Get her a glass of Atlan wine. I think she would enjoy it immensely."

Kayn looked at me. I shrugged, willing to try anything. When Kayn left the room, I must have looked confused.

"We don't regenerate Atlan wine if we can help it. The S-Gen machine never gets it quite right."

Kayn returned with a glass of burgundy liquid the same shade as the doctor's. "Thank you. Cheers." I lifted my glass toward the doctor, who looked confused. "Sorry, Earth custom. In ancient times, sloshing our drinks into each other's glasses showed we weren't trying to poison one another."

That made him chuckle, but he lifted his glass. "And now?"

"I don't know, really. I think it just means—" I literally had no idea. Enjoy? Have a good day? Glad you're here? Hope you are cheerful? "I don't know. I guess we are just creatures of habit." I touched the side of my glass to his, leaned back and took my first sip of Atlan wine.

It was spectacular.

The doctor watched me, clearly pleased when I took another sip. And another. "I am glad you like the wine."

"It's amazing."

Kayn sat down on my right, his plate filled to overflowing with a pile of steamed meat of some kind, something that looked like brown rice but was three times as big, and some vegetables I didn't dare guess at. He dug in, paying me and the doctor little attention. He, too, had a glass of Atlan wine.

We were on a military ship, in the middle of the spaceday, and they were both drinking? "Don't you guys have some rule about not drinking when you are on duty?" I knew our people did. And not just military. Doctors. Law enforcement. Paramedics. Pilots. The list went on and on.

"You are correct. The commander would have our heads. But we are not currently on duty. There are others on this ship enjoying that privilege." Kayn grinned at me and took another sip of his wine. I shrugged. Whatever. I wasn't the wine police.

My lunch was quite good, the wine even better. The company? Well, was grumpy and silent the norm around here or what? The doctor's expression remained stern. After our initial interaction, he hadn't said another word.

I didn't like silence. Or waiting.

Getting impatient, are we?

Go away.

"So, where is the commander? He told me he had to work today, but there doesn't seem to be a lot of room on this ship for him to hide." When Zarren told me this was his ship, he'd meant literally. It belonged to him and the Prillon government paid for everything, anytime he asked. Must be nice to be so important. He'd told me and I still found it hard to believe that an entire planet basically gave him a blank check.

"He isn't on board."

"What? Where is he?"

Kayn spoke between bites. He was on his second serving. "Transported to TSZ. Had a meeting."

"TSZ?" I asked.

The doctor frowned at Kayn, whose mouth was stuffed full. He was clearly unable to respond. "Transport Station Zenith. It's a Coalition operated space station that serves as a hub for military and civilian commerce in this region. It's one sector over, but out here, that's practically next door."

A space station trading fort? Interesting. Since the idea of going back to my pink and gray living room was about as appetizing as the stench coming off Kayn's plate, I tried to think of what else I might do. I asked both the doctor and Kayn, who came up with nothing. Not helpful. Then, a flash of brilliance.

"I'd like to check up on your patient, doctor. How is he doing?"

"What patient?"

"The one I met when I first arrived. Oberon Arcas, I think I have that right. I assume he is still here. He looked like he needed to do nothing but eat and sleep for at least a week." Despite all that, he was one fine looking Prillon warrior. Not that I would ever tell my mate I was checking out one of his guys.

The doctor spit out his wine. "Excuse me?"

"Oberon Arcas? The Prillon warrior?"

He shook his head. "He is, indeed, still here, my lady. And he will remain our prisoner until he tells us what we want to know."

I felt like I'd just stepped into a hip deep ice bath. "Prisoner? He's your *prisoner*?"

10

Willow

Oberon Arcas, the naked, very attractive Prillon warrior, who had been nothing but polite to me when I barged in on their—what? Interrogation? Torture session?

I looked over at Kayn. "Is that why you were guarding the door? So he couldn't escape?"

"Yes."

Three on one? He must really be something if the doctor and the commander needed an Elite Hunter for backup. For one guy? And he'd been just sitting there, not even tied up. Just taking it.

You know all about that.

I was not going to dignify her with a response. But she was sooo right.

This time, the voice in my head was all me.

Don't throw up. Don't throw up. Breathe, Willow. In. Out. "Why? What does he know that's so important?" Important enough to lock another living being up in a tiny metallic room, with no comfort, no bedding. Starved. Bruised. Cold. Naked. He'd been *naked*.

Like me. Resigned and hopeless. *Like me.* Didn't bother to fight because it never did any good.

We fought him, just not physically. Don't you dare deny us that victory.

Okay. She was right. I never stopped fighting him inside my head, no matter how hard he tried, or how much telepathy he shoved down my proverbial throat, I always managed to hide a little part of myself from him. Always.

Oberon was fighting, too. Except it wasn't some Hive Nexus psycho keeping him locked in that room. It was *my mate* and this...doctor. A fucking doctor. What happened to the vow not to do harm? That weirdly named oath new doctors on Earth had to vow to uphold. The name escaped me. Sounded like *hippopotamus? Hippa-crap—something?* Shit, what was it?

Hippocratic Oath.

Right. This guy needed to read it. Memorize it.

"He knows the location of a secret Hive facility. We need to know where that facility is."

"Why?" Was that what was drawn on those plans and diagrams Zarren stared at for hours on end? A Hive facility full of Nexus units? If that was the truth, I'd go torture the information out of the bastard myself.

"So we can destroy it."

That made sense to me. Better to kill them all, as far as I was concerned. Every warrior who'd faced the Hive probably felt the same way. Which meant Oberon should hate them as much a everyone else. So? Why didn't he want to tell them? Something didn't add up. "I assume a Prillon warrior would want them all dead. Why won't he tell you where it is?"

"Because he believes his sister is a prisoner there." The doctor spoke without any emotion. He could have been talking about the color of the table, or what he ate for dinner last week.

I was numb, the quiet inside me complete. *She* was waiting. Coiled and ready to strike me dead for being so damn naïve. I'd been so careful. This couldn't be true, couldn't be happening.

"Does the commander know about Oberon's sister?" Surely not. Not my Zarren. He would *not* leave a young woman under Hive control to suffer and be experimented on. Be forced to *breed*. Carry unwanted, parasitic life inside her body? Freeze and starve in turn? He wouldn't. He couldn't. I'd *felt* him, his emotions. He was honorable. Truly dedicated to protecting the people on every planet. The need to save everyone consumed him.

"Of course, he knows. We tried to tell Oberon; his sister is already dead."

"Did you find her body?"

"No. We sent Hunters. In addition, the facility appears to be heavily fortified. Even if we believed she was a prisoner, a rescue mission is not feasible."

No body? Big deal. That didn't mean a damn thing.

"So what is? Feasible, I mean?" Tell me something good, Doctor Man, so I don't throw up your fancy Atlan wine.

"The only viable option is to locate the facility and destroy it."

"What about the prisoners on the inside? Oberon's sister? Is she the only one?" She couldn't be, not if this location was anything like the one in which I'd been held. There had been over thirty of us. Only twenty-seven still alive by the time they found us. Five infants had, by some miracle—or curse—survived.

Not one of them mine. Thank god. No one knew what the Hive DNA and integrations were going to mean, once those kids got a little older. If I was one of their mothers, I'd be terrified.

"We do not know. There may be other prisoners."

"Then get them all out." One plus one equaled two. Light was the opposite of dark. Hive prisoners—like me—needed to be set free. Simple.

"I'm sorry, my lady. Commander Helion and I agree. Destruction of the base is the best option. If there are any prisoners still alive, which is highly improbable, it will be a kindness, I assure you, to end their suffering. The Hive scientists can be merciless and extremely cruel."

He was fucking telling *ME?* In that patronizing tone? Like I was a stupid little girl who didn't know any better.

I stood so quickly I had to grab Kayn's shoulder for balance. The doctor looked up at me as if confused.

Asshole.

I threw my entire glass of untouched merlot in his face and walked out the door.

Once in the corridor, I turned on my heel and walked back the way I had come. I was surprised to realize I'd already memorized the layout of the ship and could easily navigate the path from our quarters to the medical room—or should I say prison cell, to the cargo hold, crew's personal quarters, command center, as well as the transport station. Benefit of a small ship.

Safely inside my pink and gray hell, I pulled the drawings the commander had spent so much time studying out of the storage drawer, rolled them up tight and tucked the paper tube under my arm. Time to go have a talk with the prisoner.

In less than five minutes I stood facing off with Warlord Razmus. He stood, his back to the door behind which, I now knew, was a Prillon warrior who refused to give up on his sister.

"Get out of my way, Raz."

"My lady, I cannot—"

"Get. The-fuck. Out. Of. My. Way." I'd come back with an ion blaster if I had to. I had full access to the S-Gen system, including weapon synthesis. Never thought I'd use it, but I would, if I had to. Next time I saw Queen Jessica or Prime Nial, I was going to give them bear hugs. She'd pleaded our case and he'd understood. We needed to feel safe and in control, know for a fact that no one could ever lock us up with a verbal command. I had the highest level of access there was, except for the Prime's family and closest advisors. Higher than any *commander's*.

I'd never been more grateful.

I didn't turn around when I heard footsteps behind me, just held Raz's gaze. "Let her in. She knows everything. And he won't hurt her." Kayn walked up to stand just behind my shoulder. "If nothing else, he is an honorable male. Maybe he'll talk to her."

The Atlan shook his head, then moved out of the way. "This is a mistake. Helion will have our heads."

They were talking about my mate, the fabulous, sexy, *protective* commander I'd spent the last three days fucking non-stop. I'd trusted him because I'd believed he was something he clearly was *not*.

The door to the small, metallic room opened. I stepped past Razmus, stopped with my back blocking the entrance so they wouldn't immediately follow me inside, and issued my command. "Authorization Willow Baylor, Prillon Prime." The ship made a slight pinging noise to acknowledge I'd been heard by the system and the ship was listening. "Lock the door."

The door slid closed and sealed behind me. There he was, naked once more, perched on the edge of the hard metal platform that I'd assumed was a bedding area. A gorgeous Prillon warrior. Still—*large*—everywhere, not that I was looking. Okay, only a peep. Still too skinny, cut up and bruised. Were those new cuts? What the hell had they done to him? It had been three more days. *Three days.* While I'd been wrapped in a silk robe and sleeping in a new, big bed, having sex. And more sex.

Worried about silly nightmares like a silly little girl.

No. Stop it. Guilt spiral. I couldn't go there. Deep, dark rabbit hole with no bottom. I'd fall and fall and fall, like *Alice in Wonderland*, but I'd never find my way home. Not that I had a home. Not after this.

Damn it. I walked to the S-Gen machine and set the rolled up plans down to rest against the wall. "Coalition uniform, Oberon Arcas, Prillon Prime, include boots." I tapped my foot with impatience as the small device took several minutes to produce the clothing and boots. Apparently, a—I looked at the insignia on the uniform's chest—pilot's uniform was much more complex to create out of thin air than pajamas.

God, I'd been so stupid that day, walking in here, thinking I was playing queen of the manor. *Oh, dahlings, pweese get the pretty man some food and a blankie.*

Disgusting. I wanted to scream at myself for being so naïve, so trusting. So blind.

Keeping my face turned away so I wouldn't stare at his body, I held out the clothing.

"What are you doing, my lady?"

"Is it true? Is your sister inside that Hive base? Their prisoner?" I shoved the pile of clothes at him again, shaking them in midair so he'd take the hint.

"Yes. I believe it to be so."

"Helion and the doctor think she's dead."

"So they have said."

"You don't believe them?"

"A convenient lie. I will believe it when I see her corpse."

That was my kind of protective. "How old is she?" Breeding age, I was sure, but I wasn't sure what that meant for Prillon females.

"Amalia is twenty and six."

Shit, she was younger than me. Amalia. Pretty name. I wondered if she had the same gorgeous coloring as her brother. "How long have they had her?"

"I don't know for certain. She disappeared just over three months ago."

"And you think you can rescue her?"

"Or die trying."

That, ladies and gentlemen, was all I needed to hear. No woman—alien or not—was going to sit naked, in a cage, while some Nexus asshole tortured her body *and* her mind. Not while I was alive and could do something about it. "Put those on. We're getting out of here."

"Excuse me?" The weight disappeared from my arms even though he sounded suspicious. "Is this Helion's newest trick?"

I scoffed. "No. Not a trick. When was the last time you ate?"

"I don't know. Two days?"

I was going to literally kill Commander Zarren Helion if I ever saw him again.

The thought made me so furious I couldn't contain the emotion.

Don't you dare cry. I told you this fantasy land of yours wouldn't last.

I know. Just, be quiet. This is hard enough.

Back at the S-Gen machine I ordered what I'd heard Kayn order—with seconds. Had to be good, didn't it? Behind me, I sensed a change in Oberon's movements. He had completed dressing and bent over to put on his boots. I brought the full plate of food and set it down next to him on the torture chamber's sorry excuse for a bed. "Will this work?"

"Yes. Thank you." He lifted the plate and began scooping large mouthfuls of food into his body as quickly as possible.

"You don't need to rush. And you can have more, as much as you want." I'd locked the door. No one was getting in here until I said so. Not even the commander of this ship.

"Who are you? Really? And why are you doing this?"

Reasonable questions. "My name is Willow Baylor. I'm from Earth. And a little over eighteen months ago, I was rescued from a Hive facility. I was a prisoner there for a couple years. Just like your sister."

The utensil stopped halfway between his plate and his mouth as his striking yellow eyes focused on me, solely on me, with too much knowledge behind them. "My lady—"

"Shh. Doesn't matter. I survived. She will, too." I shook my head. "And don't call me that, please. Call me Willow." If I never heard myself referred to as *Lady Helion*, or *My Lady*, ever again, that was just fine with me. Ignoring unpleasant memories was one of my specialties.

Yeah? How's that working out for you now, sweet-cheeks? Wasn't Coalition forces that came for us either, was it? If it were up to them, we'd still be with that blue fucker.

Shut. Up.

But she wasn't wrong. We'd been discovered accidentally during one of their missions. They hadn't come specifically to rescue us; they'd been tracking down Nexus 5 through his connection to Danika and her mates. Finding the prisoners on the Hive ship had been pure chance. No one had even been looking for us. Why not? Probably because someone like Helion—no, probably because Helion himself—had refused to try a *not-so-feasible* rescue mission.

I'd spoken to Danika about that day more than once. From what I could tell, the Coalition would do just about anything, if it meant a chance to capture a Nexus unit alive. Rumor was, they'd only managed to do it once. Hundreds of years of war, and they'd only caught one of those blue bastards? Piss poor track record, if you asked me.

"I appreciate the food and clothing, my—Willow, but we will not get off this ship. The I.C. operators here are all highly trained and deadly."

My mind went to Kayn and Razmus. I'd met a few others, but they weren't the ones standing on the other side of the door. What about the doctor? Yes. He was a piece of work, hopefully still wiping wine out of his burning eyes. The other two seemed perfectly reasonable. Maybe I could talk to them, make them see how wrong this was?

"Lady Helion! Open this door at once!" The doctor's voice exploded through the comm system, flooding the room with hostility as a loud, angry pounding sounded through the door.

Or not.

"Oh, shit." They'd been listening. Ugh! "I always forget that part." Hands on hips, I took a deep breath and tried to ignore the panic setting in over the magnitude of what I was about to do. "Cease all comms and monitoring in this room.

Go dark." That was the command I'd heard given during some of our debriefing sessions on Prillon Prime, after our rescue. I'd asked Queen Jessica about it, and she'd told me it was a total shut-down of all security and monitoring in that location. Sound. Video. Everything. The ship would erase the fact that I'd ever stepped foot in this room. The command was saved for things that needed to be truly private.

The ship's comm made a ping noise. "Shut down complete, Willow Baylor. The room is dark. Is there anything else I can do to assist?" Not going to lie, sometimes I loved the Coalition Fleet's super advanced artificial intelligence system. The hub was somewhere under the surface of their planet—or so they officially said-- and it connected all their comms and transport systems throughout the entire fleet. I'd heard whispers that the system was in a stealth vessel orbiting one of their moons. Who knew? Didn't matter as long as I could talk to my friend.

"Yes. Private comm, high security, Lady Danika Arcas, Prillon Prime."

"Initiating." I counted to three. Four.... Ten. "Connected."

My friend's voice came through the comm implanted behind my ear, clear as a bell. I nearly burst into tears. I missed her. A lot. "Willow? Is this really you? Why can't I see you?"

"Danika, it's me. I had to do a direct comm. I don't have a screen. I am here with Oberon Arcas. Your mate's cousin?"

"Yes. He is. But he's a pilot on Battleship Karter. I thought you were matched to Commander Helion?"

"I was. We aren't on the Karter. But we are going to transport directly to--?" I looked at Oberon, waiting for an answer. "Well, where do you want to go? Where do we need to go to save your sister?"

"Zeus. Battleship Zeus."

"Did you hear that?" I asked. "Battleship Zeus."

"Yes. But I don't understand. What's going on?"

I watched Oberon's face as I told my friend the one thing I knew would get us the help we needed, even if she had to go directly to Prime Nial and beg. "We have the location of a Hive prison base. Amalia Arcas is one of the prisoners. Oberon and I are putting together a ReCon team to get her out."

"Oh my, God. Amalia?"

"Yes."

"Shit, Willow. Thomar and Bastion are going to go ballistic." She went quiet and I had a feeling she was communication with her mates. "Ummm..." I heard the hesitation in her voice.

"What? What's wrong?"

"Thomar is furious. He wants to know why Oberon didn't tell them as soon as he found out about Amalia. He's really upset. She's been missing for a while."

That was not a question I could answer. I looked at Oberon. "Well? Why didn't you tell your cousins about Amalia finding the base?"

Oberon rubbed his forehead. The action did nothing to remove his frown. "Our family just had our honor restored. Thomar is on Prime Nial's war council. I didn't want to take the chance that Prime Nial would discover what I was up to and order me not to go."

"You went AWOL anyway. What difference did it make?" I asked.

"I risked my honor, my freedom. Not his. Not the rest of our family's. They have all suffered enough."

"Plausible deniability, huh?" This Prillon warrior had just gone up another level on the honor score as far as I was concerned.

"I do not understand."

"Never mind. Doesn't matter. You were protecting the rest of your family." I crossed my arms and sighed, anxious to get this done. "Did you hear him, Danika? He said he was protecting Thomar, and he was afraid Prime Nial would tell him not to go after her."

"Yes. I heard." Danika sounded frustrated. I wondered what was being said in her telepathic conversation with her mates. "Thomar will explain to Bastion. He is angry as well."

I didn't have time for family drama. Now that I'd committed to this course of action, the need to get *off this ship* was like a worm gnawing away at my insides. Every moment I lingered hurt a little bit more.

"Danika, tell your mates we are going to need a ReCon team, armed and ready to go, and a ship." I looked at Oberon, who had set aside his plate. He nodded, looking at me like I was a unicorn. "We'll provide precise coordinates of the Hive base once the team is assembled."

"Okay. Be careful. Keep your comm open in case they need to reach you." I heard her mumbling to herself and remembered she was part of the only known set of Prillon mates who had full telepathic communication, thanks to some Hive experiments that nearly killed all three of them. "Thomar says Bastion is coming."

"Like I said, we'll be on Battleship Zeus. You can reach us there. Transporting over in about five minutes. Willow out." I ended the call. The banging on the door escalated, changed to exploding blaster fire. Or was that something even bigger? A cannon? Did they make ion blasters that big?

Of course they did. Probably for spaceship battles. *Pew! Pew!*

Whatever it was, the door was turning red from the heat.

"How do you expect us to get there?" Oberon stood to his full height. Fully clothed in what I realized was his battle armor, he was every bit as forbidding—and huge—as Helion.

A week ago, I would have thought about nothing but getting him naked.

Now that thought made me want to beat someone with a baseball bat—and we all knew exactly who that *someone* was.

"Watch this." I returned to the S-Gen machine. "Two personal transport beacons, coordinates set for arrival on Battleship Zeus. High priority." That last would make sure we were bumped to the front of the line, in front of cargo or anything else that could wait. Sometimes their supply deliveries took hours.

The knowledge of their transport protocols floated at the front of my mind, ripe for the picking. Guess I really had learned a lot about Prillon ships from those educational videos. Heart? Broken. Apparently, for better or worse, the mind still worked.

I rocked back and forth as the small, triangular buttons appeared side by side. I lifted them gently—no sense activating them before we were ready. "Here. One for me and one for you."

I held his ticket to freedom in front of me, the small item resting in the center of my palm. I expected him to take it. Instead, he dropped to one knee before me and bowed his head until his forehead rested against my palm.

"Willow, I am yours. I owe you a life debt and will come

when you call, render aid whenever ask, and be loyal to you from this day to my last day."

Uh oh. I didn't mean—this wasn't what I wanted. I just wanted to make sure those poor women, no matter what planet they were from, weren't left to suffer—or worse, blown to bits by my *former* matched mate.

Thankfully, Oberon stood without expecting a reply, took the beacon and attached it to the uniform covering his chest. I grabbed the drawings that had caused Helion so much frustration, held them tightly under one arm, and issued one last verbal command. Every word hurt like razor blades slicing up my throat. Damn him.

Are you sure about this?

No. I'm not. You're the one always telling me to stop hiding from the truth. You know what he did. He was going to leave her there. Leave all of them there. I can't...I just can't...

Okay. I wanted to keep him. This fucking sucks.

She was telling me?

"Willow Baylor, Interstellar Brides' Program, terminate match to Commander Zarren Helion. Bride rejects the match."

The voice that responded sounded entirely too cheerful for a task that was literally tearing me apart inside. "Matched Mate, Commander Zarren Helion. Matching protocol terminated. Unsuccessful match. Confirmed. Processing new match—"

Oh *hell,* no. I knew what that stupid bride program was trying to do, match me to the next best Prillon. My next best match.

As badly as this one had turned out? No, thank you. Makayla had been right after all. I'd been foolish to trust a computer to tell me who to love. Or not love, as he'd insisted.

"Cancel processing. Remove Willow Baylor from program database. Terminate matching protocols." Technically, that wasn't allowed. But I could do a lot of things I wasn't supposed to be able to do. Like free prisoners from my former mate's ship.

"Authorization code?"

"Authorization Willow Baylor, Prillon Prime." Took less than a second for the computer to analyze my voice command and frequency. Everyone's voice had a unique frequency. How cool was that? Another bit of useless knowledge acquired watching Coalition vids.

"Protocols terminated. Willow Baylor has been removed from the Interstellar Brides' Program database. Be advised, deletion is permanent."

"Excellent." I should have been relieved. Happy. Right? So why did I want to curl up on the floor and cry for a month?

"Willow." Oberon held his large hand out to me, the understanding and compassion on his face somehow made this tragedy hurt worse. "I'm sorry. We need to go." He tilted his head toward the metal door. I turned to see the door had begun to melt, rivulets of molten metal slid down the inside surface like melting wax.

I placed the beacon on my chest and nodded. I took his hand, his strength an anchor I didn't want to need—but did —as, with a nod of agreement, we activated transport.

11

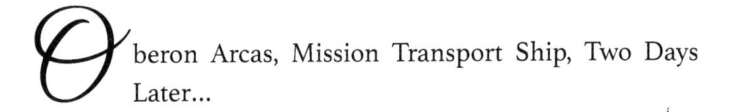

Oberon Arcas, Mission Transport Ship, Two Days Later...

HELION WAS AN IDIOT. A total fucking idiot.

His former mate? The human female, Willow Baylor?

Fuck. I wanted her. I didn't just want, I was obsessed. Wouldn't allow her out of my sight. Not only did she not have a family collar on for protection—which meant every fucking unmated male on the battleship was watching her as closely as I— but she was beautiful. Courageous. Fierce. Kind.

Fuckable. The scent of her wet heat had haunted me from that first day, when her pussy had been wet and hot, ready for her mate. I'd spent long hours staving off hunger by envisioning feasting on her, licking and tasting every part of her. Fucking her. For hours.

The knowledge that she belonged to Helion had fueled my power to resist him and his manipulations. She was an Interstellar Bride. I had figured out that much. How any female could be matched to the infamous Helion was beyond my ability to comprehend.

Why Helion would want her?

That was easy enough. Intelligent, sensual, soft and curvy, resilient.

I had hoped she would not be attached to him after such a short time. At least that's what I had assumed when she had deliberately rejected the match.

Since arriving on Zeus's ship? Her gaze did not linger on any male. Her body did not respond when she was near the others. She tolerated my presence, nothing more. She would, at least, converse with me. Look me in the eye. The others? She would barely look at any other male on the ship, as if the very sight of a Prillon warrior caused her pain.

The fact that she trusted *me*, chose my company, was a boon I would not ignore, nor take for granted. Willow Baylor was a perfect female, in every way. She should be mine.

She *would* be mine.

Fuck that asshole and his stupidity. He'd obviously hurt her, broken her heart. I knew he was a bastard. His reputation preceded him everywhere he went. But he was also honorable, or at least I'd believed, before he had chosen to leave my sister to die at the hands of the Hive in that base.

If I was going to woo Willow properly, I needed details about her relationship with Helion. I doubted she would be willing to share. I needed to know everything that had happened since she had given me clothing and ordered them to feed me.

In truth, Helion's torture had been half-hearted at best. His pathetic attempts to intimidate or harm me? Easy to ignore. I'd faced far worse on the battlefield. Even Doctor

Mersan had seemed tired, rather than dedicated to the task of breaking me.

I would have forced them to kill me. My death wouldn't have mattered. The moment Helion's ship had overtaken my small cruiser, I'd sent word ahead to the Atlans I was working with to attack the Hive base without me. They, too, knew the location of the base. They were the ones who had given me the plans, who discovered that my sister was among those taken. I would have gladly died rather than give Helion the power to destroy the Hive base while there was the slightest chance my sister remained a prisoner inside its walls.

I understood Helion's logic, could even respect it. The Elite Hunters were highly skilled. I could not believe they were infallible. I had to believe Helion would have made a different choice if it were *his* sister being held captive. For Helion the matter was simple math. The number of potential lives on one side of the scale vs the number who might die on the other. For me, Thomar, and Bastion? The decision was based on love. Family. Honor. Loyalty.

If that was not worth dying for, nothing was. Absolutely fucking nothing.

Thanks to one brave, beautiful female, our odds of saving my sister had gone from terrible to possible. With the assistance of the ReCon team Bastion and Thomar had assembled—all volunteer—plus the Atlans and their stolen Hive ship? We were now a formidable force.

Everything had changed. Once we rejoined the Atlans at the rendezvous point, we would finalize plans and initiate the rescue operation. Amalia would be saved.

When Helion captured me, that had been the *only* thing I cared about.

Until now.

Until *her*.

"Come on, O. Get your fucking head in the game." Bastion Arcas, my cousin and best friend growing up, taunted me from his side of the sparring matt. We'd been grappling for close to an hour and I was losing. Badly. Didn't fucking care. Wasn't even breathing hard.

But then, staring at a beautiful female took very little effort. "You're cheating. All those integrations made you what, twice as strong as you used to be?"

Bastion laughed. "More." His gaze sharpened and the smile disappeared from his face. "What's your problem? You should be putting up more of a fight. You're distracted."

"Trying not to hurt you." I gave him attitude, but we both knew he was right. Even now my gaze traveled across the training area to where Willow sat watching a group of Atlans try to best one another in a shooting contest. Their aim on a normal day? Deadly.

Today, not one of them had managed to hit the target, each shoving or tackling the competing beast in turn. Flexing. Roaring. Laughing. They tumbled atop one another like young boys. Every moment of their display directly in front of Willow.

Bastion kept talking, as if I were paying attention. "Oberon, we'll get Amalia out of there. I promise you."

"I know." The strike team we would take into Hive space was unlike anything ever put together by the Coalition. A group of mercenaries who happened to be integrated Atlan beasts, Bastion and myself, plus an experienced ReCon team that was made up of talented members from both Battleships Karter and Zeus? Incredible. That ReCon team, to my shock, included two humans.

One of them female, Chloe. She was a high-ranking commander in the I.C. She appeared to be small and helpless, but I knew better when the warriors from the Karter treated her with both respect *and* caution.

Even more impressive, she was the commanding officer in charge of the mission. I didn't ask how she had managed to even be part of this team, when she answered to Helion. Didn't know, didn't care. She was, according to everything I'd heard, beyond deadly when it came to infiltrating Hive tech.

Like Willow, she was from Earth. But unlike Willow, Chloe was mated to one Prillon and one human—the latter, a ReCon captain called Seth—was here with her.

A human male and a Prillon warrior shared a female? That seemed a strange match indeed. Perhaps, if we survived this mission, I'd ask them how the fuck that had happened.

Between now and then, all I could think about was Willow. She sat still as a statue, watching the Atlans fire countless shots with their ion blasters. She looked beautiful, but breakable, fragile as glass. The dress she wore was made of a fabric containing alternating, very thin, bright yellow and white stripes. A few scattered green leaves decorated the curve-hugging bodice and hem. Her boots looked soft and were lined with fur, the darker green a near match for the leaves on her dress. I knew her eyes were blue, but I strained to see them from this distance.

I could see her lips, however. I wanted to—

Bastion's foot slammed into the side of my jaw. I fell to my side, adjusting my downward momentum into a roll so I came up on my feet.

Damn. That fucking hurt. I glared at my cousin. "What the fuck did you do that for?"

"Because you are an idiot. She's beautiful and without protection. You obviously want her. Make your claim."

"I cannot. Not yet. If I move too quickly, she will refuse me." The lady—no, she didn't want to be called that. *Willow* was not ready for a mate. Even now, the smile she gave one of the Atlan acrobats before her did not reach her eyes. Her golden hair was pulled away from her face into one of her strange weaves, the look too contained for her. I wanted to march over there, loosen the hair from her braid, and kiss her until she begged for more.

Did no one else see the truth in her eyes as she watched their farce of a training session? The pain?

The longing?

Longing for what?

Gods be damned, I hoped that look wasn't for Helion. Did she desire one of the Atlans? Had she already chosen another?

Her attention shifted to a variety of practice weapons laid out for use.

Did she want to pick up one of the blasters?

I looked closer. Her hands were in tight fists where they rested atop her thighs.

Did she want to fire the weapons? Could she do so? The strange, wistful look on her face made me believe, perhaps, she could indeed. But that didn't make sense either. Everything about her was delicate and feminine. The obsessive need to protect her even more a fire in my blood because of her apparent vulnerability.

Perhaps it was her softness that had made her a match for Helion.

And perhaps it was the look I saw on her face now, the wildness she kept hidden, that caused her to end that match.

"By the gods, you are hopeless." Bastion walked to stand beside me as I rubbed my jaw. He turned to observe the

Atlans making fools of themselves to gain her attention. "I know the timing is bad, and she's already been through hell. But if you don't claim her, someone else will. You're lucky one of those beasts didn't decide she belonged to him already."

That was the fucking truth. Once a beast decided an eligible female was his mate, he didn't listen to reason, and he didn't fucking share.

Me? I welcomed another male to ensure the happiness and safety of a mate, as long as he was honorable, and a brutally efficient killer. No one would ever hurt Willow again. When she'd told me she'd been a Hive prisoner, just like Amalia, I'd seen the darkness behind her eyes, the pain. No one would ever so much as insult her. If she were mine. Which she was not.

Bastion elbowed me in the ribs and reached into his pocket. He pulled out two mating collars and held them out to me. "Go. Claim her."

"Not yet. She rejected her matched mate and removed herself from the brides' database. She does not want a mate."

"Fine, but I think you're making a mistake." He held out the mating collars, both black. "At least offer her the protection of the Arcas family. She's going to cause a riot soon if you don't do something. She has no one else. Unless she is under the protection of our family, we won't be able to stop anyone else from taking advantage of her. If you don't take care of it, I will. You know as well as I do that an unprotected female is fair game for every male who is looking for a mate."

Fuck. I knew he was right. Had I not just been thinking the same thing?

I looked around the training room with new eyes and

noticed the area was abnormally busy, especially for a ship this small. Every single training space was full to bursting with warriors, most bare from the waist up, showing off for the only available female on the ship, hoping to gain her interest.

Fuck that. It was only a matter of time before one of them made a move and claimed the right to woo her for thirty days. Kiss her. Touch her. Care for her. Hold her. Seduce her.

If one of them did, I would be helpless to stop them. Not fucking happening. She'd been through enough. I'd pledged my life to her, a life debt, for setting me free. I was worthless as a protector if I didn't stop what I knew was an impending disaster.

Beyond that, I couldn't bear to see her with another male. She was mine. I would wait until she was ready, but no one else would touch her. By offering her the protection of the Arcas family, I could care for her, watch over her. Seduce her. With our family safeguarding her, I would have all the time I needed to woo her and earn her trust.

"Thank you." I took the collars from Bastion's hand and tucked one into my pocket. The other belonged around Willow's neck.

"No problem. Danika loves her, which means Thomar will have both our heads if anything happens to that female and he has to deal with a distraught mate." Bastion chuckled but I knew his words were true. Thomar and Varin were both possessive, protective males. As they should be.

With a nod, Bastion left me standing alone, staring.

At her.

Would she despise me for this? Would her anger at Helion push her to make a foolish decision? If she did not accept the protection of the family, I would be forced to push the matter and make a claim now. I did not want to force her hand, but I wanted my collar around her neck, not for the family. For myself.

Fuck.

Willow

My feet were warm inside the lined boots. The dress I wore was pretty, but functional. My belly was full and I'd had as close to a full night's sleep as I ever did these days. I was also free of obligation to my *former* matched mate. I had a team of Prillon warriors and Atlan beasts on the way to save Amalia and the other prisoners. Everything was a win.

Except for the one, indisputable fact that I missed Zarren. I missed our connection. Could I live with a man who had decided to let all those women—Prillon or human—suffer torture, and perhaps death, at the hands of the Hive? No. Did *he* love *me?* No. Had no intention of doing so. Ever.

So why did leaving him behind hurt so much? Surely, I didn't love him. I couldn't, not after just a few days. Right? That would be crazy. Bat-shit crazy. Illogical. Foolish.

I waited quietly, giving *inner me* a chance to come out and argue, convince me that I didn't love Zarren, didn't really miss him. That I had done the right thing.

Her silence was deafening.

"What do you think, my lady? Which of these marks is closer to the center?" One of the Atlans pointed to a couple of the display screens scattered around the small shooting range. Their two, competing targets, clearly displayed. Difficult to believe, but two of the Atlans had actually managed to hit their targets. *While wrestling?*

Even you can't do that, hotshot.

The answer to their question seemed obvious, but I pointed to the winner's target because they'd asked, and I didn't want to be rude. "That one."

"*YES!*" The Atlan, who was the apparent victor, let out a roar and began to shift into his beast.

I watched, fascinated. I'd seen one or two Atlans in full beast mode since we'd transported to Battleship Zeus, but never *during* the change. My breath caught in my throat as he gained a full head of height over the others—all of whom were already giants. His shoulders grew, as did his chest. His thighs became large as tree trunks. Even his face changed, from a handsome—if large—man's, to a caricature of himself. Bigger jaw, cheekbones, eyes. Even his hands—why was I so obsessed with men's hands? —grew until they looked large enough to pick up one of Farmer Spearman's prize-winning pumpkins with one hand. *Jeeeezus.*

The beast was watching me watch him with a bit too much interest. Did I want an Atlan beast as a mate? All up in my business? Hell no. I left what I *thought* I wanted behind. Obviously, I'd been wrong about that one. I wasn't ready to jump in feet first, not again.

Was this ache in my chest all about the sex? Because good Lord, Zarren excelled in that area. I'd never had so many amazing orgasms in my life.

Sadly, no. Sex was just sex. I missed *him*. Which really sucked. I'd only known him for a few days, but the Prillon mating collars, our mental connection, made those days feel like months. I knew him better than I'd known anyone else in my life. At least, I thought I had. Maybe it wasn't *him* I missed, per se.

I missed *feeling* like he felt. Confident. Strong. Untouchable. Now that I was alone inside my own head again, I was none of those things.

You used to be. Stop fighting me. Let me out, you fucking coward.

No. Stop. You're the one who got us into this mess.

I watched the latest wrestling match between two different Atlans as they began a new shooting competition. I couldn't determine if any of them were good or not. The targets at the opposite ends of their firing lanes appeared to be untouched, but with the good-natured pushing and shoving going on, it would take exceptional skill, or a miracle, for one of them to hit the target this time.

They really needed dividers between their firing lanes, rather than lines marking the floor.

If they would give me one of those blasters, I could hit the center of that target every damn time. *If* I was willing to break the promise I'd made to myself and pick up the weapon.

My hands curled into fists where they rested on my thighs as I argued with myself.

I'd made that vow—to never pick up another weapon, never make myself a target—under duress, when I wasn't thinking clearly. When I was being sold by one group of evil aliens to another.

But—thinking clearly, and charging headfirst into danger, was what had landed me in this outer-space, alien infested mess in the first place. If I didn't have a sidearm, I wouldn't suffer from the illusion of safety. I wouldn't be tempted to do something stupid and recklessly charge into danger. *Again.*

But—I hadn't been *stupid*. I'd been doing my job. A job I'd loved, up until the moment those alien criminals from

Rogue 5 had swooped down on top of my squad car with that spaceship.

But—if I hadn't loved my job so much, I might have let things be when I couldn't find anything of note in that farmer's barn. I wouldn't have gone out searching for what I later found out was a handful of other human women who had, in fact, been trapped in that barn prior to my arrival. The fanged fuckers from Rogue 5 had tied the ladies up and left them while they waited for their shuttle to swoop down and pick up their human cargo.

They'd been too cheap to pay for transport beacons. I could order one from the S-Gen machine whenever I wanted, still had the one that took me off Zarren's ship in my pocket. But Rogue 5 was not part of the Coalition Fleet. They had to steal the few transport beacons they could or buy them on the black market. Thugs. Evil. They were pure evil.

If I wanted to make a fortune, I could print out a couple dozen of the transport beacons and sell them myself. Too bad I was a cop, not a criminal.

You used to be. Now you're a coward.

I'm not. You wouldn't have survived in the hell hole without me.

And you won't survive out here for much longer unless you let me out. You can't pretend to be something you're not.

And what is that?

You know.

I was so lost in my argument with myself I didn't notice Oberon's approach until he sat down on the bench next to me. I jumped, startled.

"Apologies, my—Willow. I did not mean to frighten you."

"It's okay. I wasn't paying attention." This was stupid. *I* was stupid. I shouldn't need an alien's psychic collar to feel like a reasonable person. It was just that I'd loved not feeling afraid all the time. Anxious. Weak. It had been so long since I'd felt strong and confident, I had completely forgotten that version of myself. Having that part of myself back had been amazing. Like waking up from hibernation and shaking off a heavy layer of ice and snow. For the first time in a long, long time, with Zarren, I'd begun to feel like myself.

Could I be like that all the time? Really?

I missed *her,* the old me. She had loved to play and go out with friends. Loved to laugh. Loved competition and adventure. She'd loved *life.*

I'm right here. Just make the fucking decision. Let me out.

I'm afraid. The admission made me want to scratch my own eyes out. Scream in frustration.

I know. It's okay. We got this. What did mom always say?

Be afraid, and do it anyway...

Yes.

Life was for adventure. I'd believed that fundamental truth for as long as I could remember. When I was seven, I tied a cape around my neck, climbed multiple trees and tied ropes around at least one limb belonging to several large oak trees in the park. Why? Because I was determined to swing from tree to tree like Tarzan.

I taught myself how to ride a bicycle when I was eight. I didn't have a father around to do it and my mother worked two jobs. I'd had to figure out a lot of things myself. I fell. I got up. I scraped elbows and knees, twisted my ankle, and had a sore ass. But I'd learned.

I saved up and bought a pair of rollerblades when I was nine and promptly zoomed around the neighborhood. I crashed and broke both wrists the week before school started. Showing up to the first day of school with two casts had made me instantly popular. The emergency room visit had earned me a lecture about the importance of wrist guards. I healed. I never wore them. Too hot and sweaty. I preferred taking my chances.

When I was ten, I'd punched Andrew Horton—who was a grade ahead and a lot bigger than me—in the nose during recess. He'd dropped a wet worm down my shirt and smashed its guts into both my skin and my favorite sweater.

That one still made me mad. That sweater had been a birthday gift from my mother. She had taken me to the yarn store, let me choose the colors, and she had crocheted it herself. Yeah. Should have punched him harder.

All those events were in the past. Long gone. My mother was dead, killed by a mugger my senior year of high school. She was the reason I joined the police academy the week after I graduated from high school. I didn't really have any family left on Earth.

I had thought I would have a new family now. Becoming a bride was supposed to be a new adventure. Bride testing had not been an easy decision for me. But I knew going home wasn't an option. My life on Earth felt like a hundred years ago. I wasn't the same woman I'd been when I was taken. Not even close.

But—I wanted to be. I was so tired of being anxious and afraid. Always waiting for the other shoe to fall.

Oberon gently touched the back of my hand. The contact with another being shocked me out of my inner monologue.

"I will make myself known next time."

That shouldn't be necessary. I should be aware of my surroundings at all times. Alert.

I shrugged. "No problem." I didn't have anything else to tell him except that he looked gorgeous, like really freaking beautiful. His cousin, Bastion—also one hot-as-hell Prillon warrior—had taken one look at Oberon when he arrived on Battleship Zeus and insisted Oberon go straight into a ReGen Pod. As a result, Oberon looked like he was completely healed. His light brown skin and hair practically glowed with health. Full, powerful muscles rippled beneath his uniform every time he moved. He was strong. Gentle. Calm compared to Zarren's storm.

"Willow?"

"What?" I looked directly at him, into those golden eyes that saw too much, knew too much. I never should have told him that I'd been a prisoner. Now he would always look at me like he was right now. With concern. Pity.

That look was the main reason I hadn't told Zarren about my past. Give me rage, or fear, or even pain. Not pity. *Anything* but pity. All pity did was make me feel even weaker and more miserable. I didn't need any help in that department.

Oberon's sigh made the hair on the back of my neck stand on end. Whatever he was about to say, I wasn't going to like it.

"I do not know if you have been paying attention, but there are more than a few warriors in this room."

"Yes." There were. Every matt was full. "I assumed they were all getting ready for the mission."

His deep chuckle was pure amusement, and contagious. I smiled, despite my melancholy mood. "These warriors do not need to train. Most of them were active on assignments until we left Zeus. They are in peak condition, I assure you."

Inspecting the hand-to-hand combat, wrestling and practice with various weapons going on all over the area. I was confused. "So, what? They're nervous and blowing off steam?" That made sense. Sitting around waiting for bad things to happen was the absolute fucking worst.

"No. They are all here, every single one of them, trying to impress you."

Oh shit.

He cleared his throat as if what he was about to say was even worse. "The males in this room are all unmated. Since you rejected your match to Commander H—"

"Don't say his name." I pressed my fingertips to Oberon's lips to stop the flow of words. His hot, full lips. The second I realized I was staring, I yanked my hand away as if burned.

God, I really was pathetic. Why couldn't I control myself around him?

Because you know he is honorable. He would never betray your trust.

Shut up, obnoxious me. Go back to sleep, or wherever you were.

Too late for that.

I knew it was true. Being mated to Zarren had changed me, made me remember what if felt like to be strong, whether I liked it or not.

Oberon. Focus on him. He's talking.

"I do not wish to upset you. I pledged myself to you, vowed to protect you. That is why I must insist you wear this." He held out his hand. I looked down to see a mating collar.

"Are you fucking kidding me right now? No way."

12

Willow

My outburst drew the attention of the Atlans, who turned as a group to watch the interaction. I knew enough about them to know that if Oberon threatened me in any way, he wouldn't live to regret it. But why was he doing this to me?

I should want to slap him across his handsome face. So why had my heart done a silly little flip in my chest? Was I completely insane? I'd been sitting her about to cry over Zarren, and now I was swooning with Oberon? Next level. Really. I had to get myself together. "I do not want a mate. I just got rid of one."

Oberon placed the ribbon in my open palm and closed my fingers around it. "I am not claiming you as my mate. I am offering you the protection of the Arcas family. You are young, beautiful, and unmated. Were you a Prillon female, your family would protect you until the day you chose to remove your collar and announce to the world that you were seeking a worthy mate. You do not have a Prillon family to protect you. Nor an Atlan family. Under Coalition law, you are unclaimed and unprotected. Any of these males could stake a claim on you, Willow. They could take you away from me for thirty days, and I would not have the right to stop them."

He was right. I'd lived on Prillon Prime for over a year. I knew their laws. Hell, I'd read the laws governing mating in general, and the bride matching protocols in detail. Every word.

An Interstellar Bride could reject her match at any time. But a normal Prillon female walking down the street? They were protected by their families until they were ready to find a mate. When that happened, they would remove the collar themselves and wait, mingle, meet people. If a warrior was interested, he would claim her and put *his* mating collar around her neck. After that, he had thirty days to win her over. Seduce her. Make her fall in love.

During the thirty days, the warrior fought to win her heart. If he failed, she would move on at the end of the thirty days and meet a new potential mate. Repeat, ad nauseum, until she was settled and happy.

I wasn't wearing a collar. I didn't have a mate or a family to protect me.

God. I might as well have a target on my back.

A shudder of ice-cold dread ran the length of my spine. I'd been lucky, so far, that the shirtless warriors on this ship had, up to this point, tried to get my attention before staking their claim. Judging by the concerned look in Oberon's eyes, my grace period was running out.

"I—thank you. I haven't been thinking clearly since we escaped." As far as I was concerned, getting away from

Helion before I'd fallen *completely* in love with him, qualified as an escape.

"May I?" Oberon held out his hand once more, this time so that I could give the collar back to him. The moment felt surreal, like it wasn't really happening.

I turned, angled my knees to point away from him, so he would have access to the back of my neck. His hands wrapped around me as he took one end of the collar in each before lifting them to either side of my neck. His skin was hot where he grazed my neck and I had a strange sense of Déjà vu. Except last time, it had been my hands lightly touching the skin of Zarren's neck, moments before our minds had connected.

Oberon's touch lingered at the base of my skull, or perhaps I imagined it. The collar locked into place and adjusted to my neck like an elastic band.

Or a noose.

As Zarren had done, I reached for the collar and ran my fingertips along its smooth surface. I felt nothing. There was no psychic connection, no intense blast of desire. No power. Just me.

I was still alone in my head. Which was what I wanted. Wasn't it?

I turned around to face Oberon and discovered him staring at me with a look I could not decipher. "Thank you."

His gaze locked with mine. "I will always protect you, Willow. It is my honor to do so."

Why was his voice strained and unhappy? Perhaps he regretted his whole *I-owe-you-a-life-debt* vow. So why did I want to crawl into his lap and ask him to hold me? Worse, why was I disappointed that I could not? Why was I thinking such things when I knew I could not possibly be what he would want in a female? Oberon was from a powerful and influential family. He did not need to settle for a sad Earth girl who was already in love with someone else.

God damn it. I didn't want to love Zarren, but I did. What a disaster. All of it.

"I release you from your vow, Oberon. I don't want you to be stuck with me for life just because I gave you some clothes and a transport beacon. That hardly seems fair and wasn't my intent."

"I do not accept your offer. I will honor my vow."

Before I could protest, Oberon changed the subject completely. "I saw the longing in your eyes when you were watching the Atlans."

"What?" What was he talking about?

"You have trained with a weapon, have you not?"

What the—? "How do you know that?"

He lifted one hand to cup my cheek. "I do not need a mating collar to see you, my lady."

He made the title—*my lady*—something intimate. Special. My heart raced like a hummingbird's as his thumb moved back and forth across my cheek. I didn't realize I'd started to cry until he wiped a tear from my cheek.

I sat, glued to the seat, to him. Somehow, his touch had become an anchor. I couldn't move away, didn't want to. How did he know something I'd never told a soul who wasn't back on Earth? Was I that transparent? Was he truly interested in me? In who I was? What I wanted? The thought was both sobering and scary. If he saw me this clearly without a mating collar, what would it be like to share that bond with him as well?

What did he feel like? Zarren had been power and rage. Dominant and demanding. *Hungry.* What would Oberon's emotions feel like inside me?

"How long has it been?"

I knew what he meant. "Since before—"

He knew exactly what I referred to. "Ahh." His gaze broke away as he looked over to the firing lanes.

Reluctant to look anywhere but at him—how embarrassing, crying in front of all these warriors and beasts—I finally turned my head to find the entire training room was now empty.

One little-bitty collar around my neck and, suddenly, no one needed any more practice? God, they really had been here to try to impress me. All of them. Even the Atlans.

I'd been so wrapped up in Oberon, I hadn't noticed them leaving.

Terrifying.

"Were you any good?" Oberon stood slowly, one hand wrapped around mine so he could coax me to my feet.

"Yes. I was. I'm a country girl." Not lying. I'd competed in shooting competitions since high school, and visited both the indoor and outdoor range at least once a week the entire time I'd been a cop. Ten years. I was damn good.

He looked confused for a moment, then dismissed the thought and raised one brow. "Do you think you can beat me, Willow Baylor, country girl from Earth?"

Sassy me, the old me I'd tried to bury deep down in my soul, shot up out of her seat, and whooped with joy.

I was tired of fighting her. She was stronger now.

I was stronger.

"Yes, I can." Screw the Hive. Fuck Nexus 5. Fuck every second of every day I'd spent in that hell. That had just been my body. Not *me*.

Not my soul. The past was done wrecking me, holding my soul hostage. I couldn't do it another minute. Not one damn second.

My connection with Helion unlocked the cage I'd built

around myself, the protection, the illusion I wove for self-preservation. Oberon had seen the real me crouched in the dark, hiding inside. He saw through my disguise. Somehow, he recognized things I had refused to acknowledge myself.

Fuck yeah. I was going to do what I wanted to do from now on.

Sassy me and scared me came to an understanding in that moment.

I couldn't put her back inside the cage. The very thought threatened to suffocate me. I was free.

I dashed to the door, more excited than I'd been in ages. Even more excited than when I'd been processed as a bride. "Just a minute. I'll be right back."

I raced to my tiny, private room. I had an S-Gen there, barely big enough to make my clothing. I stripped naked. Top to bottom. I didn't want a single stitch of docile me's clothing to touch my skin. I was done being meek and agreeable. Inoffensive. Careful.

Never again.

I shoved the dress and boots into the recycling unit and stood in front of the S-Gen machine.

"Coalition battle uniform, Willow Baylor, include boots."

I could barely stand still as I watched the clothing appear. When it was ready, I slipped on the pants and top—built in bra for the win—and took a nice, long look at myself in the mirror. Checked out my backside. Turned this way and that.

Bad. Ass. I looked like a superhero. The uniform fit me like a glove, every curve I had hugged tight and put on display. The fabric was made to block blaster fire, as well as ensure survival for several hours in space, but it was light and flexible. The pattern was odd, not quite what I would call camouflage, and a mix of silver, gray and black.

"Ion blaster with thigh holster, sized and coded to Willow Baylor."

"Willow Baylor, place your hand on the scanner for sizing."

The computer had never heard this request before. I thought about it. Guess I'd never made myself a pair of pretty gloves.

I put my palm down on the black and green grid. A soft glow lasted less than a second.

"Thank you. Remove your hand."

I did so. I moved around as I waited. Jump. Kick. Squat. Twirled my arms around in big circles, forward and back.

Nothing bunched or squeezed. This uniform was *fantastic.*

A few minutes later—apparently weapons took even longer than uniforms to create out of thin air—or raw energy particles—I picked up my newly issued, Coalition sidearm and matching thigh holster. Grinning like a kid on Christmas morning, I put the holster on and slipped the new, sleek, silver weapon into place. The weapon's grip fit my hand perfectly, created and sized specifically for me. My DNA would have been coded to the weapon the second I picked it up. It was mine. No one else could use it. Ever. I slipped the transport beacon into my pocket—not letting that thing out of my sight.

One more look in the mirror.

Not quite there yet.

Reaching for my hair, I pulled the elastic tie loose and then ran my fingers through the braid to unravel it. When that was done, I flipped my head upside down, shook my hair, roughed it up with my fingers, and flipped my head back up to inspect the results.

There I am.

The woman staring back at me was a wild thing. Confident. Strong. Ready for anything.

I didn't take more than a quick peek. One, I'd start crying—sobbing, blabbering, snot-bubble crying. Two, I'd been gone for a while, and I didn't know if Oberon would still be waiting.

Of course he will.

I looked down at my chest, curious about the strange insignia on my uniform. I had no idea what it was, but it looked cool. Contributed to the whole *Bad-Ass* theme I had going.

Feeling more like myself than I had since before I'd been captured, I made my way back to Oberon. If his slack-jawed shock was any indication, I looked as amazing as I *thought* I did.

I laughed out loud—another shocker. Not a fake laugh, forced laugh, ha-ha aren't you amusing laugh. A *real* laugh. I didn't recognize the sound.

"Let's go, hotshot. Show me what you've got." I walked to the nearest firing lane and activated the warm-up program. I was a bit rusty, but within a few minutes, I had made friends with my new blaster. I hit the target dead center. "Like riding a bicycle."

Oberon took position in the lane next to me and activated his program.

I watched him warm up, more than a little curious.

Shit. He was good. Really good. I wasn't sure if I could beat him.

You've got this, hotshot.

This time, I didn't argue with that sassy little voice. This time, I smiled.

"Best two out of three?" Oberon grinned back at me. Clearly, he had zero intention of letting me win just because I was a girl.

My entire body sizzled with anticipation. This was going to be *fun*.

Zarren Helion, Battleship Zeus, Sector 438

I wrapped Willow's mating collar around my hand and closed my fingers into a fist. This should be around her neck. Where it belonged.

My *mate* should be back on my ship, safe, in my bed... where *she* belonged.

This fucker knew where she was and wouldn't tell me.

"Go home, Helion. Go sneak around in the dark and do your job. There is nothing for you here." Commander Zeus had taken over patrolling this sector of space when the previous battlegroup had been destroyed by a new Hive weapon. He'd challenged for his position, beaten the other warriors—despite being half-human—and cleared the sector of Hive threats with an efficiency even I admired. He was single-minded, driven, and completely uncompromising. Exactly like me.

"Tell me where she is. I know she was here. Bastion Arcas transporting to your ship the day Oberon escaped was no coincidence."

"I don't know what you're talking about." If he weren't a battleship commander, I'd be tempted to kill him. Fuck that, if anything happened to Willow, I *would* kill him. If not for

Zeus, I'd already be at her side, keeping her safe, making her see reason.

"Chloe Phan? She's mine, you know, part of the I.C. And Seth Mills, her mate? One of the best ReCon captains in the fleet? They all arrived on your battleship within hours of each other."

Commander Zeus leaned back in his seat and put his boots up on top of his desk. "I don't know anything about them. They sound like great assets to the Fleet."

Fuck. Me. I couldn't sit in front of this arrogant asshole's desk for another minute and practically *beg* him for information. I stood. Couldn't make myself leave. Palms flat on Zeus's desk, I leaned over his pathetic barrier and looked him in the eye.

"If anything happens to my mate, I will kill you."

Zeus stood and mirrored my position, our faces so close I could see the very human roundness of his pupils. Like Willow's. Even this asshole made me think of her.

"I'm going to give you a pass just this once. You are obviously distraught over a female you love. But if you threaten me again, you will die of old age in my brig."

Fuck. He could do it, too.

"Please." I was begging. By the gods, I was fucking begging. What was *wrong* with me? I did not beg. Fuck that, I didn't even *ask*. *Ever*. "Please. I need to find her."

Need. That was the correct word. It wasn't the new furniture or the way her body wrapped around mine that drove me. I missed everything about her. Voice. Scent. Passion.

I missed the way she listened. The depths of her compassion. The resilient, steady anchor of hope in her mind. I didn't know if she was aware of that part of herself, but there was something inside Willow that was unyielding in her joy for *living*. Stronger than anything I'd ever known, her true power lay hidden like a secret treasure inside a small, beautiful, breakable female.

I'd never told her any of this. Like a fool, I'd taken her for granted. Soaked in all of her strengths—hope, acceptance, kindness, compassion, love—fuck, I'd known she was falling in love with me—and kept her to myself.

She should have had a second immediately. I should have asked about her nightmares the first night she trembled in my arms, not waited until guilt gnawed at me. The truth was, I'd been a fucking coward. Afraid to share her for fear I'd lose her heart to another. Afraid to ask about the shadows inside her because I didn't want the fantasy life I was living to end. I should have faced her fears with her, not pretend they didn't exist. I'd hidden the truth from myself.

It was my fear that held me back, not hers. Afraid to fail her. Afraid she would wake up and realize I used duty as a shield so I wouldn't have to *feel*. I'd fucking failed her in every way, except one. I loved her. I'd sworn not to, been arrogant enough to fucking *tell her* I would *not* love her. For one reason, fear of what was happening right fucking now.

She was the only thing I cared about. The *only* thing. I would destroy anything or anyone who tried to keep her from me, who *hurt* her.

Like I had. I fucking hated myself, but I couldn't let her go. I would spend the rest of my life on my knees, begging forgiveness, if she would give me the chance. She. Was. *Mine.*

"Please. I need her."

Zeus tapped the ends of his fingers against his desk, the movement quick and agitated. "Let me explain this to you one more time. You're a smart one, I'm sure you'll understand. You do not have a mate. You *had* a mate, for less than a week. Now you do not."

"She is mine."

"*She* says she's not. She rejected the match, as is her right. Move on, warrior. Find another female."

"There is no other, not for me." I stopped hiding my desperation, allowed what I was feeling to show on my face. In my eyes.

He studied me for nearly a minute, then sighed. "Then you are fucked, Helion. Prime Nial himself locked down their mission brief. Even I can't see it. If I liked you, which I don't, I might be tempted to take pity on you just to watch you drop to your knees and beg that beautiful female to give you another chance. I can't tell you where she is because I don't know. No one fucking knows." He sat back down. "Now, get the fuck off my ship. I have work to do."

I'd used every trick I had, called in every favor. It was like she'd disappeared into thin air. No record of her transport. No mission logs. There was one mention of a comm call between my ship and the capital. *One.* The security clearance needed to view the details were above mine.

Which meant Prime Nial was involved, as Zeus claimed, and I was fucked. If the Prime had locked down the information, nothing could break through, no program, hacker, or insider I had at the capital. If Prime Nial was protecting her, I wouldn't find her until he allowed me to do so.

If he allowed it at all.

Nothing existed in the records that even mentioned her name—except the fact that she'd refused her match to me.

That was in the fucking records. She broke our match and removed herself from the brides' database. Small comfort that she couldn't be matched to anyone else. The fact that she'd gone with that Arcas bastard—helped him escape—had me seething. But that wasn't the source of the stabbing pain behind my ribs. No, that sharp, stabbing agony was my long dead heart—and it wasn't so fucking dead after all.

I would get nothing here. I didn't bother to say good-bye, knew Zeus would neither expect nor welcome another word from me. He'd made his position clear. He knew I had fucked up. He knew Willow was beautiful, which meant she *had* been on his ship, and he had, in fact, seen her himself. He knew she had refused our match.

He knew Prime Nial had personally locked down all information about where she was, what she was doing, and who she was with.

Desperation was not an emotion I enjoyed. At the moment, it crawled through my veins like fire slugs burning me alive from the inside out.

What if she chose another mate before I found her? What if she would not listen to me? Refused to give me a chance to explain? To beg her forgiveness for not caring for her properly, having no second, pretending she was not hurting or suffering nightmares?

I had replayed her conversation with Oberon hundreds of times, heard the catch in her voice when she told *him* what she had not shared with me. Her mate. Her protector. Her lover.

I should have fucking asked.

Perhaps, if I had asked, Willow would have told *me* that she had been a prisoner of the Hive. I would be the one holding her right now, comforting her, protecting her. I would be the one she turned to when she was hurting or alone.

Not *him*. Fuck. Oberon Arcas was a Prillon warrior in his prime. He was probably speaking to her at this very moment. Touching her. *Listening* to her. *Wanting* her. Plotting a way into her bed.

Gods fucking help him if he hurt her.

The only thing keeping me sane was the knowledge that Oberon was an honorable male—and a skilled warrior. He would neither hurt, nor force his attention on, any female. He was skilled enough to protect Willow. Judging by his devotion to, and willingness to die in a hopeless attempt to protect his dead sister, Amalia, he would fight to the death to keep Willow safe.

I just hoped he was not equally determined to keep her for himself.

I made my way to transport. Several minutes later, I was back aboard my small, lonely fucking ship. The moment I was alone in the command room, I sent a comm request to the only other person who *might* be able to help me. Within moments, a beautiful female's face appeared on my view screen. Dark hair. Gray eyes, as always, full of hate. For me. A hate I deserved.

"Warden Egara."

"Helion, what is it this time?" Her gaze narrowed as she studied what I assumed was an image of me on her side of the conversation. "What happened? You look like shit." That was Catherine, straight to the point. Her observation was not surprising as I had neither eaten nor slept since Willow left me. I'd been too busy looking for her... and berating myself.

"I need your help."

"One of my brides in trouble again?"

"Yes, a bride is in trouble." My bride. My mate. *Mine.* I would beg this female to help me if I had to. Pray she did not hate me enough to deny me.

She sighed and shifted in her seat so she could work on one screen and speak to me on another. "Okay. Who is it this time? Where is she? Give me details." This was not the first time we had collaborated to help a human bride. This was the first time either one of our requests to the other was personal.

"Her name is Willow Baylor."

Catherine frowned. "Hmm. I don't recognize the name. I don't think I processed her. I assume she is from Earth?"

"Yes. And no, you did not. She was--"

"What the hell?" Catherine, my brother's mate—at least she had been, before I'd gotten him and his second killed—looked at me with round, shocked eyes. "She was *yours?*"

"Willow is mine."

"Not according to this. She rejected the match? In less than a week? No second?" Catherine's gray eyes locked onto mine through the screen. "And now her location and all personal information has been locked down by Prime Nial himself? Holy shit, Zarren. What the hell did you do?"

Zarren. No one had called me that in years, except Willow. My Willow.

I told Catherine the truth, about the day Willow had arrived, about the prisoner and why I'd held him here. The reason I'd chosen to destroy the base, rather than risk more lives—like I had before. I even repeated Willow's conversation with Oberon when she had helped him escape—at least what I'd heard of it before she locked us out and went dark.

"That's all peripheral. What did *you* do to *her?*"

"She was upset about the prisoners and Oberon's sister. I didn't know she had been a prisoner. I should have asked her or told her about Oberon myself."

"No. That's not enough to make a woman leave like that. What was going on with you two, before that? What did you do to hurt her?"

I couldn't make myself admit my sins aloud. "So many things."

Catherine sighed. "You told her your bullshit line about not ever loving her, didn't you?"

"I--" How did she know?

"God, help us. No wonder we still haven't won the war."

"What does this have to do with the war?"

"Apparently, we have idiots in charge."

"Are you calling me an idiot?" What the fuck? I'd called her for help, not to be derided and insulted. No one spoke to me this way. Ever.

"I am. And you are." She leaned in close to her comm so that her face filled nearly my entire screen. "Listen to me. Really fucking listen, Commander. Can you do that? For once?"

When I remained silent, she continued.

"I blamed you for a long time, brother. I even hated you for a while. But I realized a while ago that you have hated yourself even more." She turned her face to the side and wiped a tear from her cheek before looking squarely into her comm. "This has to end, for both of us."

Brother. She had not called me brother since before I'd given the order that sent her mates to their deaths. Before I'd realized not every battle could be won, that numbers would defeat intention every fucking time.

"Zarren, I forgive you. I forgive myself for hating you. I forgive *them* for going on that mission when they *knew* they would probably die. You told me, right after their deaths, that you never wanted to make another decision based on emotion. That you would never love again. You truly believe you have done exactly that for the last seven years. Don't you?"

"I have."

"No. You haven't. I can't believe it took me this long to figure you out. The opposite is true. The exact opposite. Every single thing you've said or done since your brother died was driven by your love for him. *Everything* you have done, every decision you've made, was based on that love. You have hated yourself, closed yourself off, refused to speak to me, and god only knows what else, because you loved him. Because you *still* love him."

The violence and rage I kept locked deep inside, the fuel I used to survive the months and years of loathing and guilt, didn't explode inside me, they transformed.

No. *This* was what they had been all along. I'd simply refused to look behind their disguise.

Agony. Despair. Grief. *Pain* filled me up, bubbling up inside me like water from a hot spring. I had bathed every cell of my being in its weight, soaked my soul with it for the last seven years, held onto it so there wouldn't be room for anything else.

No space for fear, doubt, personal desires, longing, forgiveness. Love.

Until Willow merged her heart with mine, shared her emotions with me.

Forced me to live. Forced me to *feel*. Now I couldn't fucking stop.

Catherine sighed, shaking her head. "Do you love her? I mean, really love her? Do anything to make her happy?"

I swallowed around the lump in my throat. "Yes." I swallowed my pride, my fear, my command. "Can you find her?"

As I had many times before when one of her brides—or their mates—was in trouble, I waited as Catherine worked her magic. I had warriors, weapons, and ships. She had contacts I did not. Queen Jessica, Prime Nial's mate, was hers. As were Danika Arcas and Chloe Phan. I was the head of the Coalition Fleet's intelligence operations, but Warden Egara had an entire network of contacts—her brides—who would assist her if she asked. Which I could not.

At this point, if I did ask any of those human females for help, they would probably cut out my heart, rather than help me find my mate.

Catherine should have been a spy. But then, she had been, when my brother claimed her. Fuck it all, maybe I would resign and give her my job.

"There's nothing. No one is talking. I can't help you." She held my gaze. "I'm sorry, Zarren. I wish I could help, but I can't get through. Everything is locked down tight."

"I know." What the fuck was I going to do? "Thank you for trying to help."

"You deserve love, brother. I hope you find her."

Catherine ended the comm and I sat, stunned, for several minutes. What just happened? My entire existence tilted on its axis. Catherine didn't blame me. Worse, she was right. Every second of every day my actions had been dictated by love—and guilt—over the deaths of my brother and his second—and dozens of others who had perished on a fool's errand. I thought I'd been so fucking cold and calculating, so sure I would never make another mistake, never make decisions based on emotion.

Fuck. Look at me now.

I activated my ship's comm. "Kayn, report to command."

Pacing, unable to sit still with so much helpless fear pumping through me—fear that I'd lost her forever, fear that she would not forgive me, fear that she would choose another mate before I could find her and tell her I loved her—

Fear that she would die because I was not there to protect her.

I was out of options, out of contacts, out of control. There was only one possibility left, one way to find my bride before it was too late.

The door opened and Kayn stepped inside. Elite Everian Hunter. The best I'd ever seen. I'd been confident enough in his skills to tell Oberon his sister was dead. Ironic that he was now my best, and only, hope.

"Commander?"

"We're going hunting, Kayn. And we're starting now."

13

Oberon

Two out of three became three out of five. Four out of seven. After a while, we stopped keeping track.

I was certain Willow Baylor, *country girl,* and, I'd learned, law enforcement officer back on Earth, was the perfect female.

That discovery had come hours ago. Now I tried to keep my mind focused on the game we played, rather than all the ways I wanted to touch her. Kiss her. Taste her.

The row of cards she'd placed face up in the center of the table, as well as the large stack of something she called chips next to it, had her laughing. She called this game poke her. Poking who, I wasn't sure. Nor had I figured out what these colored betting chips had to do with physical assault. I waited and played the game, assumed at some point the poking part would come into effect.

The only thing I truly ached to do was *poke* Willow's pussy with my cock. No, not poke. Slide in deep, wait to hear her gasp, her moan of pleasure, pull out and do it again.

Maybe I would taste her pussy every few thrusts of my cock.

Maybe I would feast on her pussy and then slide my cock into her eager ass. I did not know what her former mate may have done to prepare her for a second. Perhaps she liked to be taken there. I could wrap myself around her, fill her from behind and fuck her pussy with my fingers.

Or—

Bastion kicked my foot beneath the table.

"What the fuck?"

"Are you playing this game or not?"

Not. I was busy fucking Willow in my mind. Apparently, I was taking too long to make my play. I was nearly out of betting chips, as was Bastion and several others we had lured into the game. Willow laughed.

Gods be damned, I could listen to her laugh for hours. Which was how long my cock had been hard and hurting.

"I do not believe this game is real. I think you created it to torment us, female." A massive Atlan scowled at his few remaining chips.

Chloe and her mate, Seth, both laughed. The human male spoke. "Oh, poker is real. But if I'd known Willow was from Vegas, I would have kept my money in my pocket and walked."

"What money?" Chloe leaned to her side and bumped her mate with her shoulder. She was a beautiful human female, with long black hair and dark brown eyes. But not as beautiful as Willow.

We had another day of travel before the rendezvous with

the Atlans and their hijacked Hive ship. I had no doubt her mate would like to spend the entire time pleasuring his female. As would I.

We finished the hand, Chloe taking the 'pot'—although there was not a cooking utensil in sight. She leaned her head against Seth's shoulder and yawned. "This was fun, but I'm wiped."

"Are you asking me to take you to bed?" Her mate appeared to have no resistance to her request. I understood the feeling. She wasn't mine, but if Willow asked, I would provide. Anything.

The two humans said their good-byes and left our quarters. The Atlan surrendered his final chips to Chloe, grumbling the entire time. He bid us goodnight as well. That left three of us in the room.

Bastion and I had been assigned a small space. Two narrow beds in two attached rooms, each bed barely large enough to hold one of us. For a small ship, when one included the table space we occupied while playing the poking game, our quarters were unexpectedly spacious.

Which meant we'd been assigned the extra room to accommodate our newest family member, the female now legally under my—our—protection. Mine, and Bastion's and Thomar's. Thank the gods. I would not have slept if she were elsewhere on the ship, vulnerable to whichever aroused male believed it a good idea to seduce her.

Which is exactly what I wanted to do.

Willow began gathering the cards and chips, stacking everything into an unknown order. There were dark circles under her eyes. Now that things were quiet, and Willow wasn't hosting her human companions, she looked frail. Weary.

Considering the transformation I'd witnessed today, she should be exhausted. Soft, feminine, fragile Willow was beautiful. Warrior Willow, as she had dubbed herself after our targeting competition, was irresistible. Sexy. The Coalition uniform she wore accented every curve, from hip to breast, and I wanted to explore all of her. For hours.

Bastion took one look at me and excused himself, taking the small sleeping room nearest the entrance. Good. That left the right for Willow. There was no need for Bastion to ask. We both knew I would be sleeping on the floor outside her door.

If I wasn't invited to her bed.

"You are tired. Go. Sleep. I will finish this." I waved my hands over the table and the items still scattered on top.

"Thanks." Willow stood and walked toward her tiny bedroom, then stopped to look at me over her shoulder. She smiled at me with a tenderness I had never seen before. She didn't hide her fatigue, or the gratitude I saw in her eyes. "Oberon, thanks for today."

"It is my honor to serve you."

The small smile faltered, and I wondered what I had said wrong.

"Right. Life debt and all that." Her smile returned, but the matching softness was missing from her eyes. "Well, thank you anyway. This was the most fun I've had in a long time."

Afraid to say something else that might offend, I simply nodded and watched her until she closed the door to her room. Everything we'd been using to play her strange game went into the recycling unit. I laid down on the floor with my back pressed to her door. She was here, with me. She was safe.

I slept.

WHAT THE FUCK? Something wasn't right.

I didn't move, didn't so much as twitch. Slowly, I opened my eyes to scan the room for intruders. My instincts raged at me to get up, fight, eliminate the threat.

Silence.

The room remained quiet as I lay there, listening.

There.

A whimper. A soft cry of anguish.

Willow.

I reached for my weapon and moved into a crouch along the wall next to her bedroom door.

She cried out again, softer this time. More like a sob.

Whoever was in that room, hurting her, was going to die a slow, agonizing death.

Fuck that. I'd rip their head off. Sometimes, faster was better.

I waved my weapon in front of the sensors and held my breath as the door slid open with a very soft, swishing noise.

I braced for attack.

Nothing.

With one powerful movement I leaped into her room and scanned the area for threats.

There was only Willow, still dressed in her uniform, boots on the floor next to the bed, ion blaster peeking out from under her pillow. Her body was curled into the smallest, tightest ball she could manage.

She shivered, as if freezing. The room was not cold. I'd made sure of that when Bastion and I discussed sleeping arrangements.

"What the fuck?" Bastion's course whisper came from

behind me. I spun to find him in a nearly identical stance, weapon ready. "I heard her. What's wrong?"

I shook my head and answered in a nearly imperceptible whisper. Bastion would hear me, the incredible number of Hive integrations in his body not only made him stronger, they amplified his natural senses to an incredible level. "I do not know."

We both stretched to our full heights in the dark and put our blasters away, careful not to make a sound.

"Is that a blaster under her pillow?"

"It is."

"What female sleeps with a weapon?"

I sighed. Perhaps one who had been captured and tortured by the Hive. A female with a mate who had betrayed her. One who did not feel safe.

Rather than give away Willow's secrets—she had not mentioned her captivity to anyone else as far as I knew—I shrugged. "She was a law enforcement officer on Earth. She told me she carried a weapon. She is very skilled. Better accuracy than most warriors."

"What?" Bastion looked at her, where she lay curled up on top of her bed and whispered back to me. "She's too small. What idiots would allow her to risk her life in such a manner? No criminal would fear her."

"Ask Captain Mills. His mate is small as well, and serves in the I.C."

"Humans do not make sense to me." After another long look at Willow—who whimpered yet again—he lifted his eyes so our gazes met and held. "Take care of her."

He turned and left the room. The door slid closed, sealing me inside as a new, tangy scent filled the air. Salt? Tears?

Did Willow now cry in her sleep?

Careful not to wake her, I slipped the weapon out from under her pillow, made sure she couldn't kill me before she knew what she was doing, and put it back in place. I wanted her to feel safe, not threatened by a hulking Prillon warrior looming over her in the dark.

No, looming was not what I intended. But I could not bear to hear her suffering. Nightmares haunted all of us, especially those who had seen battle.

I crouched down until my face was nearly even with hers and whispered her name in the dark. "Willow. Wake up."

Nothing. She cried out, the sound an agony in my soul. If I ever found the Nexus unit who had captured and tortured her, I would tear him apart piece by piece.

"Willow. Wake up. You're dreaming."

Nothing.

Fuck.

I decided to risk a gentle shake of her shoulder.

At first contact Willow bolted upright, her weapon in hand and pointed directly at me. I froze. "Willow, it's Oberon. You were dreaming."

"Shit." Shaking now, she lowered the weapon to the bed next to her hip and ran one trembling hand through her sleep tousled hair. She had never looked more beautiful. "I'm sorry."

"I am not." I watched her for long minutes as she attempted to regain control of her emotions—and failed. Her tears did not stop.

Willow was not my mate. I did not have the advantage of sensing her emotions through a mating collar. But I had many nights of practice holding Amalia, when she was small, after she woke from nightmares.

Decision made, I scooped Willow off the bed and into

my arms. I thought, perhaps, she would protest. Instead, she leaned her head on my shoulder and sobbed. I sat on her bed and leaned my back against the wall. I had no intention of letting her go.

"Tell me." My demand was soft, but unrelenting.

14

Oberon

Willow was in my arms, although not the way I had imagined.

I suspected this moment between us would be far more important than anything else we did, clothed or not.

I activated the lights, just enough so she could see me, know she wasn't alone in the dark. Not anymore.

If I survived the mission to free Amalia? Never again. She would never be alone again. I had yet to choose a second, but a few minutes with Willow and the warriors would be lining up, begging me to accept them.

Willow had suffered enough uncertainty. Perhaps I would gather sufficiently powerful warriors and allow her to choose.

"Tell you what?" So much depth behind her question. If I said the wrong thing, she would keep her secrets, try to protect me from her pain.

"Everything." Every. Fucking. Thing. I wanted to know everything there was to know about her.

She cried for a long time. When her words at last began to mingle with her tears, she described the beauty of the desert and canyons where she grew up. How she'd been drawn to becoming a 'cop'—which was one name for human's who enforced Earth's laws—when her mother was murdered.

Her grief was old, but deep. I waited—would wait for as long as she needed to be ready to tell me more.

Her breath caught as she told me about a call for help that came from a local family. They called the law enforcement team—including Willow—to investigate what the family believed were intruders on their property. Willow's tears dried as she recalled the building full of animals, but nothing suspicious.

"I should have climbed back into my car and gone back to the station. But I didn't. I saw flashing lights farther out, along a back country road."

"The lights were from a ship?" I knew what was going to come next and focused on relaxing every muscle in my body. A difficult task when all I wanted to do was hunt and kill the ones who hurt her.

"Yes. I didn't know any of this at the time, but they had taken other women and tied them up in the barn. That family was right—there was something going on that shouldn't have been. But by the time I showed up, they'd loaded their prisoners onto the shuttle."

"They should have returned to space. Not taken you."

"They told me, after they stripped me and put me in chains, that the sight of a female warrior amused them. They baited me onto that road. I was over-confident. I had a shotgun in the car, backup close, and I was really good with my pistol. I walked right into their trap."

"You could not have known you were chasing down a spaceship. Earth is not part of the Coalition. What they did is not legal, not by your laws, or ours."

"Didn't matter. I should have been more careful, listened to my instincts. I was too dependent on my uniform and my gun to keep me safe."

Understanding dawned. "That is why you did not ask for a weapon once you were freed."

"Yes. And why I made myself look—"

"In need of protection?" I provided my own answer. I did not know what she would have said, but I doubted I would approve of any word she chose. Fragile. Weak.

"Non-threatening." She began to stroke my chest with one hand. I had no idea if the action was unconscious or deliberate. Either way, the contact did not help me focus on her words —until what she said shocked me. "But you saw through me. How? No one else ever did. Not once. Not even—"

"Your mate?" She stopped petting me. I never should have mentioned Helion, but he was already in the room.

She was quiet far too long. I wondered what she was thinking. Feeling. Did she regret leaving him behind? For the first time that night, I resented the intimacy of the darkness surrounding us, wished I could look into her eyes.

"Yes. The commander. I should have told him."

"He should have asked." I was not going to help her make excuses for that selfish—

"He did."

What the fuck?

She resumed stroking my chest through my uniform. "I —distracted him." She sounded like a naughty child.

"What did you do?"

Arousal. Wet heat. Her scent assaulted me as whatever thought she had wreaked havoc on her body. And mine. My heart pounded. My cock was hard and heavy. Ready to fill her. Fuck her. Make her come.

Fuck. How was I going to keep my hands off her for two more days? I didn't want to push her, officially claim her, until the mission was over. We were going into battle. I would not claim her and leave her in a span of hours. Not after everything she had shared.

There was one vital piece of information missing. I needed to know who to kill.

"Who took you from Earth?"

"Those fanged criminals from Rogue 5."

"What color were their armbands?"

"What?"

"The males who took you from Earth. What color was the band they wore on their arms?"

She stilled. "Why?"

"There are five legions on Rogue 5. I want to know which legion I should hunt."

"Oh. I thought they were all the same."

"No. Each legion has its own laws, set and enforced by their leader."

"But they are all criminals."

"Yes. Strictly speaking, but they have a unique code of honor, and they protect their own. Two of the legions are respected by the Coalition. One is—irrelevant."

"The last two?"

"Vile. There are few limits to the evil they are capable of."

"Like a group of competing mafia families."

"I do not know this term, mafia. I only wish to know the

color they wore."

"Blue."

Siren. The next group of Siren members I ran into at Transport Station Zenith...

I envisioned rivers of blood. Screams. Fanged fuckers on their knees, begging me not to kill them—

"And then there was Nexus 5." She shivered. I dismissed thoughts of murder and wrapped my arms more tightly around her.

"Tell me."

She did, her arousal gone as quickly as it had come. Nexus 5 had been a clinical and efficient tormentor. She glossed over her suffering, but it was there, in her voice. Torture. Experiments. Pain. Despair.

The longer she spoke, the stronger her voice became, the more her tears faded, replaced by rage. Yet she did not protest as I held her. Somewhere along the way, I had begun to stroke the side of her face, alternated with sliding my hand up and down her back as I tried to steal her pain and take it into myself.

"Oberon, I'm sorry. I wasn't going to tell you any of this."

"Why would you not?" The thought of this female keeping secrets, hiding her pain from me, made me want to crush things.

"I've thought about it a lot. I realized it is difficult to acknowledge someone else's pain. It's hard to look at, because if you see their pain, you feel it, too. Like it's yours. Their pain becomes part of you." She sighed. "Even at the capital, after we were rescued, we didn't look each other in the eye."

"You will always look me in the eye, Willow."

"Why?"

"I cannot care for you if I do not know what you need."

"I've heard that somewhere before."

Helion? Again? This time, I did not ask.

"Never mind. I just didn't want to make you worry about Amalia more than you already are."

"That is not possible. Either she is trapped inside that Hive base, or she is dead. I cannot imagine anything worse. There is no need for you to protect me."

That made her smile, I felt the pressure of her bunched cheek where it rested against me. "Correct me if I'm wrong, but if it weren't for me, you would still be naked, starved and tortured on that asshole's ship."

"Perhaps."

"I'm sorry about that. I was so stupid the first day I saw you. I thought you were a patient, not a prisoner. I didn't want to see the truth."

I kissed the top of her head because it was the only place I could. I did not have the right to kiss her anywhere else. "I have suffered far worse on the battlefield. Helion's interrogation would not break a child."

"What?" She shoved against my chest and leaned back to look up at me. "He was melting your skin off."

I shrugged. "Technically, that was Mersan's doing."

"The doctor?"

"Yes. But even he grew weary of the tactic. I do not believe either of them truly wished to break me."

"How can you say that?"

"I am not dead."

She stared at me. I watched her intelligence at work as her mind fit puzzle pieces together. "Like what? What did he not do?"

I began to explain, in graphic detail—because this female was not one to hide from the truth of things—the various things they could have done to me but did not.

Broken bones. Eyes plucked from my skull and regrown. Tongue torn from my mouth and reattached. Severing of spinal nerves—regrown with the ReGen wand, then cut again.

"God, stop."

I shrugged. "Nearly any injury can be healed, Willow. Melting away some skin is actually quite pathetic, as torture goes."

"You are all insane."

I chuckled. "Perhaps. But the training we endure when we join the Fleet is far worse. He did not want the truth."

"How can you say that? I thought that was his job."

"I do not know what to say. Perhaps he is weak."

"Weak? He didn't seem weak to me."

Was that offense I heard in her voice? Did she still have feelings for him?

"Yes. He has been hiding behind a desk for too long. He is weak." I ran my palm over her back, enjoyed the feel of her beneath my palm. "I am not."

"A desk jockey, huh?" She squirmed, her soft ass rubbing the tops of my thighs. Now that she was not in pain, my cock refused to behave. I ached, hard and eager to take her.

Her hands rested on my chest. Her scent filled my head. We were alone in the dark, our faces so close I could taste her on the air. The slightest movement would press my lips to hers.

Fuck. There was no hiding from the raw need clawing through me.

"Tell me to leave, and I will do so. I want you, Willow. I want to taste your pussy and fill you with my cock. I want to make you whimper and beg and scream my name." Truth, because that was the only thing I would allow myself to give her. "I can smell your skin, your pussy. It's driving me mad."

15

Oberon

I closed my eyes as she caressed my face with one hand. Small fingertips traced my cheekbone. My brow. My lips.

"Are you saying you want to be friends with benefits?"

"Fuck no. I want to be your mate. But I will not claim you until after the mission."

"What? Why? I don't understand."

I was beyond understanding most anything. My cock was hard and throbbing, my senses flooded with her. Only her. Everywhere. The sound of her voice. Her heat. The weight of her in my lap. The light touch of her fingertips on my face.

"The mission will be very dangerous. I might not—"

"Shut up. Don't you dare say it."

She leaned forward and pressed her lips to mine.

Rising onto her knees, she wrapped her arms around my

head, holding me to her with fierce strength I now knew had been forged in the fires of fucking hell itself.

The scent of her arousal hit me like a hammer at the base of my skull. Her pussy was hot. Wet. Ready.

For *me*.

I buried one hand in her golden hair, slipped the other behind her to grip her soft, round ass. I pulled her close, claimed her with my touch the way I could not with a collar.

She moaned and leaned into me, swiped her tongue along my lips. Demanded entry.

Fuck. She was right there with me, rubbing her sensitive nipples up and down my chest. Kissing me like she'd never get enough, never stop.

"Clothes. Off."

We both scrambled off the bed onto our feet. I stripped in seconds, uncaring of what condition I might find them in later. Naked, burning alive, I took one look at my female and stopped moving. I watched her wiggle out of her uniform. Pants fell to the floor. She lifted the hem of her fitted top up, over her head. Tugged. Squirmed.

Her breasts popped free.

I was on my knees, sucking them into my mouth. Tasting. Nibbling. She still had her arms up, over her head, stuck in the tight sleeves of the fabric.

"Oberon." My name was part laughter, part arousal, and part frustration. "Help."

"I'm busy, female." I held her in place as I continued to explore her body with my mouth. Breasts. Nipples. Neck. Back down to the outer curve of her breast. Waist. Hip bone. Thigh.

"Oberon!" She laughed in earnest now. "I'm going to fall over."

I lifted her in my arms and carried her, so she lay flat on

her back, arms caught and held above her head, her knees dangling over the end.

"This feels very naughty." Her voice was shaky, husky.

"Do you want me to stop?"

"Hell, no. I like naughty." She'd managed to free the bottom half of her face from the uniform's top, her lips on display, ripe for the taking.

I crawled over her and kissed her. Hard. Soft. Deep, tasting every part of her. Nibbling on just her lips. I could have kissed her for hours. Would have, if there had not been something else I needed to taste even more.

I moved slowly, kissed and licked my way down her body, devoting time to every curve and valley. By the time I reached my destination, she was writhing, her thighs rubbing together in search of relief.

"Mine." With one hand on each thigh, I spread her legs wide, revealed her hot, wet core.

The air was heavy with the musky scent of her need. For me. Only fucking me.

I lowered my lips to her clit and sucked the sensitive nub into my mouth. Thrust two fingers into her pussy. Worked her body into a frenzy, stopped. Grinned when her back arched up off the bed, her ankles locked around the back of my head.

I needed to hear her cries of pleasure. Needed to feel her hands tangled in my hair, her grip tight, desperate.

I shifted, moved lower, fucked her with my tongue. Stabbed deep. Locked my mouth around her wet core and sucked the edges of her soft flesh into my mouth as I filled my senses with the taste of her.

Consumed. She consumed me. Without a mating collar, without shared desire.

By the gods, with that connection? Surely my heart

would explode. I would lose my fucking mind. All thought. All control.

Her pussy squeezed my tongue. Released. She deliberately tempted me to fuck her, fill her with my cock, thrust hard and deep until nothing else existed for either of us.

Not yet. Not until she gave me everything.

I moved my right hand over her abdomen, holding her down as I rubbed her clit with my thumb. My left, I slipped under her ass, playing. Testing. She thrashed, whimpered, pushed against my touch, tried to take my fingertip inside her tight ass.

Not yet.

She had stopped trying to free her arms. They remained over her head, her lips available, wet from the flicker of her tongue, body on display. Open. Submissive. Her complete surrender woke something dark and feral inside me.

I *needed*. Needed to fill her ass and pussy together, mark every part of her, claim every sigh. Moan. Whimper.

Push her body to its limits. Take her higher.

Make her scream. My name. Mine.

She was mine.

With a slowness meant to drive her mad, I slipped my hand up her thigh, over the front of her hip, down her back until my hand rested on that perfect, sexy curve just above her ass.

Slid lower. Worked my finger inside her bottom as I fucked her with my tongue, rubbed her clit faster. More pressure.

Her ankles dug into my shoulders. She tried to lift her hips off the bed, push her pussy harder against my lips.

Her orgasm stole her control. She thrashed. Her pussy pulsed. Swollen. Hot. Her cries were animalistic, so fucking hot my cock pulsed, ready to come. So close. I grit my teeth and held myself in check. Not yet. I wouldn't come until I was buried balls deep.

And she was coming all over my cock.

I knew, if she could see my face, she would not recognize the possessive creature watching her fly apart. Memorizing every detail. Licking the taste of her from my lips, eager for more.

Gods, she was magnificent.

Greedy. So fucking greedy, my lady. For more.

For me. Her mate. She was mine now. All I had to do was survive the mission and claim her.

Mine.

Willow

I couldn't breathe. Heart about to explode out of my chest. My entire body shaking, trembling. That orgasm, Oberon's tongue in my core, his finger in my ass. I didn't believe in hell, but in that moment, I knew if I was going there, I didn't fucking care.

"Oberon."

Thank god, he took the hint. He kissed his way up my body as I struggled, pulling one elbow free from the surprisingly tight shirt. I yanked it off my other arm and tossed it across the room. Arms over my head? Blindfolded by my own shirt?

Hot. So damn hot.

Now I wanted to *touch*. I wanted to feel everything I'd *missed*. Warmth. Touch. Comfort. Pleasure.

Oberon.

I wanted to feel *him*. This wasn't collar induced lust. The only thing I could feel was my body, not his. My emotions. The blood pulsing through my veins. Only mine.

Which made this urgent need to have his cock inside me completely crazy. Everything going on in my mind was jumbled, confused, and focused on one simple truth.... I would spontaneously combust if I didn't get his cock inside me as quickly as possible. I wanted *him*. Inside me. Part of me.

Everywhere.

Who was I kidding? I'd wanted him since the moment I walked into that room, seen him sitting in the chair. Naked. Stoic. Beautiful.

He sucked my nipple into his mouth, laved it with his tongue. Groaned when I buried my fingers in his hair and pulled. Hard. Aftershocks, little mini orgasms, flitted through my pussy like butterfly wings. So sensitive. Needy.

I needed him inside me, filling me up, stretching me open. I wanted his body covering mine, consuming me, making me part of him.

"Oberon."

"*My lady.*"

The way he said the words this time? Possessive. Reverent. I'd never be able to hear them without thinking of him. Of *this*.

I dug my heels into the edge of the bed, lifted my hips so I could rub my clit against his abdomen. Make him *hurry*.

He moved his attention to my other nipple, clearly not in a rush.

I tried to sit up...

He wiggled the finger he'd kept inside my ass.

My pussy clenched, on the edge of another release. I moaned, the pull on his hair changing to an exploration. Seduction. I was panting. "Please. I need you inside me."

His groan encouraged me.

"Please. Fuck me. Fill me up." I lifted my hips once more, this time prepared for the movement of his finger, eager to feel it again. "Do that when you're inside me."

"Willow. Fuck."

He was done resisting me, teasing me. Playing. I could hear the ache in his voice, the need. All I had to do was beg...

"Fuck me. I need you."

Urgency replaced his languid movements. His muscles hardened, flexed as he moved higher, his chest held like a tasty treat just above my face, his weight braced on one massive arm.

The head of his cock nudged at the opening. Rolled over. Left me. Returned.

I wrapped my arms around his back and dug my fingers into his heat. "Please."

One slow, smooth roll of his hips and his cock slid deep. Held perfectly still as his groan filled my ear and vibrated my ribs. The sound was pure pleasure and made me want to move, take him, make him mine.

Shaking once more, I tried to move. Fuck myself on his hard length.

He was stone, unmovable, completely in command, of both of us. The tension built like steam inside a kettle. He held me down, locked the lid, allowed no release.

His strength made me wild. Nothing was forbidden. Off limits.

No secrets existed between us. He knew everything, every horrible, disgusting thing Nexus 5 had done to me. How scared I'd been. How weak. He knew I'd been broken —was still broken but growing stronger.

I was finished lying to myself. This change in me had

started the moment I'd been connected to Zarren, been flooded with his strength of will, his rage.

I had chosen to be a bride knowing I would love two warriors. Be with two powerful males. Give myself to both of them.

Now I had.

No going back, only forward. I didn't have time for regrets. Life moved on. I was not going to stand by and watch.

I lifted my head and bit Oberon's chest. Not hard—just hard *enough*.

"Fuck."

He lost control, his cock moving in and out of me with a frantic pace. I locked my lips over his skin, filled my mouth with his taste as he filled me up. Pushed me over the edge.

My inner muscles exploded in a series of spasms and jolts that squeezed his cock, threated to push him from my body. In response, he pushed deeper, forced my body to accommodate him, stretch around him. My body pulsed and craved and tasted him as he pumped into my body, his release making him tremble.

I wanted everything. His skin. His taste. His pleasure and his pain.

I wanted to keep him.

And I ached for Helion.

I was so fucked up in the head. I wanted the impossible.

I wanted them both.

16

Willow

I STOOD between Oberon and Chloe Phan, the commander in charge of our mission, and watched the line of *visitors* walk out of the transport room. The small ship grew smaller with every new face.

Three Atlans. All huge. All in full battle armor. Each and every one of them with some kind of Hive integration visible. Their ship—which Oberon told me they had actually stolen from the Hive—could be seen on the vid screens, floating just outside ours, in the middle of nowhere.

I recognized their ship. I'd spent a long, long time on one nearly identical to it.

Even now, standing next to Oberon, armed to the teeth —I'd added a second ion blaster to the opposite thigh— something felt *wrong*. I couldn't put my finger on what, just a darkness creeping into my mind, making me skittish.

Knock it off. You're ruining my hot sex afterglow. Oberon

had barely allowed me to come up for air since the moment I got him naked and in my bed. Not that I was complaining.

Shut up. I know. Something isn't right.

For the last time, you are NOT cheating on Zarren. He is NOT your mate.

It's not that...

To be fair, I had spent an unhappy amount of time missing him—and arguing with myself about the futility of the situation with my commander. I couldn't stay with someone who would just leave those Hive prisoners to suffer and die. Could. Not. But no matter how hard I tried to stop wishing things were different, I kept right on grieving the fact that the dream hadn't come true. Because other than that, Zarren had been pretty damn perfect for me.

So is Oberon.

I know. I want to have my cake and eat it, too. Okay?

Good luck with that.

Mean. But inner-me wasn't wrong. Thinking about Zarren was useless, hopeless and about a dozen other exhausting, waste-of-my-time emotions.

Thank god I wasn't synced up with Oberon through a mating collar. The rough and tumble war going on inside my head was no fun for me. For him? If he were smart, he'd run as far from me as he could get.

No matter the source, the icy tingling up and down my spine was totally wrecking what should be me, dipped in nothing but happiness over my new—sexy, hot, amazing— relationship with Oberon. Instead, I was nervous. Jittery. Like waiting for the other shoe to drop, despite knowing both shoes were already on my feet, illogical, gut punch uneasy. The feeling didn't make sense.

Maybe the Atlans were freaking me out—Oberon told me there were even more of them that weren't coming over from their ship. But what about Raz? He was at least as big as these Atlans. Full armor. He hadn't bothered me at all.

I had a very strong hunch the icy edge on my nerves might be caused by the *other* guy coming out of the transport...

What the actual fuck was *that?*

Or should I say, *who* was that?

"Holy fuck." Chloe mumbled with just enough volume that I heard. And agreed. One hundred percent.

"Who is that?" I asked.

Oberon placed his palm flat on my lower back, offering warmth and comfort I hadn't realized I needed. I was feeling stronger than I had in years, but seeing that Hive ship, combined with this strange creature's presence, creeped me out. "That, my lady, is a pure-blood, Hyperion prince."

Whoa. And I thought the fangs on the Rogue 5 assholes looked scary.

Chloe—*Commander Phan*—crossed her arms over her chest and stared outright. "Someone please tell me why he is practically naked."

Boy was he ever. He wasn't ugly, far from it. He looked like a sexy, thinner faced, slightly taller, Atlan beast. Not an Atlan. A beast. The Hyperion was far too big to pass for a normal Atlan. But his features were more refined than a beast's. His chest was massive, as were his thighs. He was bare foot, which seemed ridiculous for outer space. But I guess, if he had boots on, he wouldn't be able to use that second set of claws.

He wore a pair of stretchy shorts that looked like they were made of the same material as the others' uniforms, but it only covered him from hips to mid-thigh. Modest? Hardly. They hugged his ass and—other things. The rest of his body? Bare. Muscles that went on for miles. Freaky, silver,

Hive integrations ran the entire length of his spine, from the base of his skull to where they disappeared under his barely there shorts.

All that was fine.

Two things had me pressing back into Oberon's supportive hand.

One, his eyes. They were the strangest color I'd ever seen, like lime sherbet or the soft filling of a key lime pie. Not a living green like Zarren's. Nothing living that I knew of —except maybe an insect, or a butterfly—had anything that color, *anywhere* on its body.

So, okay. Oddly intense stare from neon green eyes. But the fangs. And the *claws*...

The creature stopped mid-step, lifted his head like a bloodhound following a scent trail, and turned toward us. He moved so fast I didn't have time to panic. Oberon, however, stepped in front of me—and Chloe. Seth Mills, Chloe's human mate, was a few feet away with his weapon out and ready, pointed directly at the Hyperion who now stood within arm's reach. Too close.

"You females are human." His voice was deeper than anything I'd heard before. So deep, I could hardly believe the sound came from his throat and not a machine.

"We are." Chloe was the one who answered him. "I am also the commanding officer on this ship and will be addressed accordingly. Commander Phan. And you are?"

"Rukzi." He inhaled slowly, pulling more air into his lungs than it would take to fill my entire body. "Yes. Human. Like Cormac's Abby." His eyes narrowed as he looked from Oberon—who stood blocking his path—to me. I held my hand over the grip of my blaster, ready pull the weapon and shoot this giant if he made one wrong move.

Hell yes, I could shoot with both hands. Thank god, because Oberon had my right side completely blocked.

"Mated?" He looked from me to Chloe. "Both?"

"She's mine." Oberon made the statement publicly, despite the fact that I was not, technically, his mate. Yet.

Seth hadn't lowered his weapon. "Touch my mate and you die."

Rukzi looked at both males, then back to Chloe. "You do not command me, little female." His claws clattered together as if to emphasize his point, and I could have sworn they were twice as long as they had been before he walked over. Then again, this close, everything about him seemed bigger. I wasn't sure how that was even possible.

"Then get the fuck off my ship."

Tense silence. One second. Two. Bright green eyes bored into Chloe. Hands on her hips, she stared right back, despite the fact that she had to crane her neck back so far to meet his gaze, it looked like her head could snap off her spine at any moment.

Rukzi burst into laughter. "I want one."

Oberon grinned and his entire body visibly relaxed. "Get your own. These two are taken."

One of the Atlans appeared next to Rukzi and placed a hand on the nearly naked male's shoulder. "Stop stirring up trouble, Ruk." He inclined his chin to me and Oberon, then addressed Chloe. "Commander Phan, I'm Warlord Enzo. My ship and my team are ready."

"Excellent." Chloe glanced over her shoulder at Seth. She must have made a face at him or something because he finally lowered his blaster rifle—eyes locked on Rukzi the entire time. His blaster wasn't a small one, like the thing strapped to my thigh. Seth's rifle looked like it could do some real damage.

Enzo looked at Oberon and broke into a real smile. "Prillon, good to see you again."

Oberon held out his hand and they did the manly forearm hold by way of a greeting. "Have you been monitoring the base?"

"Of course."

"And? Any sign of the prisoners?"

The Atlan shook his head. "I'm sorry, my friend. But no. We have not been able to break through the Nexus unit's security to scan the interior."

"But the base is still active?" Chloe asked.

"Yes. They have drones patrolling their perimeter. We will not be able to sneak up on them. We will need to convince them our ship is part of their collective." He tilted his head to the side, motioning toward where he must have parked his spaceship. "Which is why we took their ship after our escape."

"You were Hive prisoners?" I blurted the question. Had a hundred more in line behind it. When? Where? How long? How had they escaped? What kinds of experiments were done to them? Bit personal? Yes. I still wanted to know.

"Indeed." Rukzi's chest heaved. "I am not yet finished bathing in their blood."

"Don't get him started, my lady. Trust me." Warlord Enzo slapped the huge Hyperion on the back.

Oh, I could just imagine...

Chloe lifted her hand and waved them along as she walked toward the largest room on the ship. "Come on, then. Let's finalize our plans. We only have a few hours."

Eight hours, thirty-two minutes. Not that I was counting.

Enzo, Rukzi, Seth and Bastion—who had been following the activity in the room where he leaned against the wall—followed Chloe. Oberon remained.

"Aren't you going to go with them?"

He shook his head and lifted a hand to cup my cheek. "No. I am a pilot, not a battle strategist. I will go where they tell me I am needed." He lifted his opposite hand and wrapped it around my waist, pulling me close. "Right now, I need to be with you."

"Oh." Could this warrior be more perfect? I leaned into his touch and closed my eyes. God, he felt good. Warm. Strong.

Without warning, a feeling like cold sludge moved in my gut, making me nauseous. I concentrated on getting fresh air in and out of my lungs, waited for the feeling to pass.

"What is it?"

"I don't know. I feel like something is wrong, but I don't know what." I turned and placed a kiss in the center of his palm. "It's just nerves."

Or missing Zarren?

No. It's not that.

You sure?

Shut up.

Oberon pulled me into his arms and wrapped me up tight. "I will not allow anything to happen to you."

"What about you? Down there in that stupid Hive base?"

"Do not worry about me. I have seen many battles. I do not fear the Hive." He pulled back and looked down into my face. "I will come back to you."

"I'm going to be really angry if you don't."

He chuckled and lowered his lips to mine. One touch and I was gone. His.

Zarren Helion

Weapon drawn, but at my side, I grimaced and forced my mind to focus on my surroundings before the final, glacial vestiges of transport faded from my limbs.

"What the fuck?"

The outburst was followed by the sounds of weapons being readied, warriors moving into position to surround me and the two I'd brought with me. Elite Hunter Kayn and Warlord Razmus stood on either side of my position.

A quick glance at my surroundings assured me I was exactly where I needed to be. We faced off with a full ReCon team, in uniform and armed, ready to fight. Small ship, stealth variety, black metal similar to the one I'd just left behind—upon which the remainder of my crew remained, ready and waiting for my command.

I was here for one reason. One. My mate.

Willow was mine. She was on this ship. And if Oberon, or anyone else, had hurt one hair on her head, I would fucking kill them first and ask questions later.

I'd told Willow I was a monster. That was, in fact, the truth. She simply had not seen that side of me. Yet.

I put my blaster away and lifted my hands over my head to wait out the startled shouts and deadly movements of the Coalition forces Prime Nial and Thomar Arcas had assigned to this mission.

They should have fucking asked me first. Seemed to be a theme, of late, assuming I didn't know exactly what I was doing.

Not the safest approach, perhaps, appearing unannounced on a ship no one was supposed to be able to find. But I had Kayn. The only beings he could not track? Dead ones.

Like Amalia Arcas, and the dozen other females who had disappeared around the same time. Kayn looked for weeks, for *all of them*. He found nothing, not the smallest trace.

Oberon had refused to listen to reason. Sentimental. I admired his dedication to his family, but not when it placed my mate in danger. He had taken my female off my ship and brought her here, to a forward operating combat vessel on the verge of launching a certifiable suicide mission. Inside Hive controlled space.

Fucking idiots. The lot of them.

"Don't move. Don't fucking move."

I knew that voice...

A human male moved from my peripheral vision to stand several paces in front of me, rifle pointed directly at my chest. He made sure to stay far enough away that I would need to think twice before rushing him. He was cautious, and deadly.

No wonder I liked him.

"Captain Mills. I assume my commander is here with you." It wasn't a question. I knew Chloe was on this ship. And she was mine, a top officer in the Intelligence Core. Why *she* had not contacted me before accepting this mission was a topic I fully intended to bring up the moment I had her alone.

"Fuck, Helion. Give a guy some warning next time." Seth Mills lowered his rifle and glanced at something behind me.

I turned to find Oberon Arcas in an embrace with my mate. Kissing her. Arms around her.

She was kissing him back.

She had a fucking mating collar around her neck.

His?

I took a step toward them before I'd even registered the

movement. Warlord Razmus stopped me with one huge hand dead center in my chest. "Careful, Commander. Real careful."

Fuck me, he was correct. I could not afford to fuck this up, not if I wanted Willow back in my life, and in my bed.

Which I did, more than I wanted to keep breathing.

I closed my eyes and called upon the deep, dark well of icy self-control I'd created—and perfected—the last few years. The darkness I had used to bury my grief. My love for my brother. I used it now to hold down the urge to rip Oberon's head from his shoulders.

"Thank you, Raz."

The giant Warlord blinked at me, slowly. "You have never called me that."

"It's what she calls you, isn't it?" I'd heard her speak to him, and about him, on multiple occasions. It was a familiar name. A name used by friends.

"It is."

I lifted my hand and covered his where it rested on my chest, holding me back from charging into a volatile situation. It was more than his hand on my chest, his word of caution. I realized my entire team had been there for me, stuck by me, stayed with me through the last few years of hell—and I'd not treated one of them as a friend. Assets. Skill sets. Tools I had available.

Never friends.

Which was fucking stupid. What was a friend, anyway? A person one cared about, helped out, looked after. Like he was doing right now. "I've been an ass, to all of you." I looked from Raz's shocked expression to Kayn, who stared at me with calculation in his eyes. Always thinking, that Hunter. Too fucking much like me. "Thank you." I squeezed

Raz's hand and lifted it away. "Thank you both. For everything."

Kayn dipped his chin in response but said nothing. He didn't want to be here. I knew why. He'd looked Oberon in the face and told him that Amalia was gone. Now, if we continued with this assault on the Hive base, we would have to deal with that Prillon's grief as well.

Not even denial was strong enough to overlook a corpse. Gods forbid we should find the remains of Oberon's sister.

Raz dropped his hand to his side and tilted his chin in Willow's direction. "Don't push her too hard. She'll run."

"I know."

Raz nodded and stepped out of my way.

Willow was *still* kissing that fucker. Her arms were around his shoulders and she was pressed, fully, against him. Her hair was down around her shoulders in a wild tangle I'd only ever seen when she ripped out one braid and began another.

Gods be damned, I don't think either one of them noticed our arrival.

They were both consumed.

What the fuck was that Prillon doing? Did he plan on fucking her right here? On the fucking floor? Because he *had* fucked my mate. I knew the way she kissed, the way she melted into her lover, the way she would wrap her arms around his head and hold him like she never wanted to let go.

My hands clenched into fists at my sides. She wasn't, technically, mine. She could fuck whoever she wanted, whenever she desired to do so.

Didn't mean I had to fucking like it.

And what the fuck was she wearing? A Coalition uniform? With full battle armor? A *weapon* strapped to her thigh? Every curve on display. Her rounded ass, full breasts, soft thighs...

His hand was on her ass. The other? Buried in her hair. His lips never leaving hers, like he couldn't get enough.

I took two steps. Three. Close enough to hear her little sigh of pleasure.

That sigh was *mine*.

Fuck. Maybe I *would* kill him.

"Commander Helion! What the hell are you doing on my ship?" The feminine voice was nearly a shout, her tone stern, one familiar with command. That would be Chloe Phan. My intelligence officer, or so I'd believed. Was feminine betrayal the theme for this week?

The loud question caused Willow to freeze in Oberon's arms. She tore her mouth from his and turned her head to find me, so close, watching her give herself to another male.

"Oh, shit."

She had no fucking idea.

17

Willow

Oh god. Shit.

Calm down. You're not his mate. Not anymore.

Okay. That was true. I wasn't his mate. He wasn't mine. I had another Prillon family's protection and a new, smoking hot warrior who was totally in love with me—and not afraid to say it. He told me he wanted me. He told me he'd never leave me.

He was a big boy and knew how to use his *words.*

Unlike *Mr. Stares-A-Lot*, who didn't even blink as I slid down Oberon's body to stand on my own two feet.

"Helion." Oberon didn't let go of me until I delicately removed his hands from around my waist and took a step back. Breathing room. I needed some breathing room here.

"Arcas." Zarren's voice was stone cold. God, I knew that voice. He was beyond angry, his gaze not lifting to mine until Oberon's hands were off my body. He'd had no problem staring at that, making everywhere Oberon's hands lingered burn with awareness.

He has no right to be angry. You didn't do anything wrong.

I could have talked to him about it first.

No. We've had this conversation. He was going to leave those women to suffer and die when he could have done something about it. What if that was you? He would have left you there, with that fucking psychopathic blue asshole, forever.

Oh, yeah.

Why was it so difficult to hold on to that outrage when he was standing here, in front of me, saying nothing?

"Willow, I would like to request an audience with you. Alone."

"No." Oberon's objection was instant. But he wasn't my father, and I was no child.

"I can speak for myself." I turned to glare at Oberon, who narrowed his eyes and stared right back. He wasn't happy about this. Well, I doubted anyone on this ship was happy at the moment. The three of us, least of all. How horrible would it be later, when we were battling the Hive? When I had to wait, knowing Oberon was out there, fighting, risking his life... and Helion was like fire burning through my blood. His anger made me want to push him harder, make him lose his temper. Make him *feel*. Something. Anything.

Make him explain why he wouldn't even try to save those prisoners.

What if he has a good reason? Maybe my former mate had an answer I could live with.

There is *no good reason, no fucking way.*

I glanced from Oberon, who was clearly fighting the urge to throw me over his shoulder and carry me away, to Zarren, whose attention was so focused and absolute it was as if he was consuming me, heart, soul, everything. Everything was *his*.

What the hell are you going to do? I didn't believe he'd come after you. This is a disaster.

Tell me about it.

I just did.

Zarren turned away from me to address Chloe, who had covered the distance and stood with one eyebrow raised, her hands crossed over her chest. "Commander, why are you here?"

"I'm here for my mate."

Chloe's gaze darted to me, then back to Zarren so quickly I thought I might have imagined it. "She's not your mate, Commander."

Zarren turned his head to the side to address me. "That is for her to decide. My lady, may I please have a word?"

Oh, shit.

You keep saying that. Stop saying that.

Zarren held out his hand, palm up, and waited for me to decide what to do.

"Do not, Willow. He will only hurt you." Oberon's voice was quiet. I doubted anyone but myself and Zarren heard his plea.

I looked up at Zarren and studied him. I'd worn his mating collar. I knew his moods, the emotions he claimed not to possess. Right now, he looked... sad.

I took Oberon's hand and squeezed it. "I'll be fine. Don't worry. I need to talk to him."

Oberon closed his eyes as if in pain but did not protest when I released his hand and walked to Zarren. I did not place my hand in his. I did look him squarely in the eye. "Okay. Let's talk."

There weren't many places on a ship this small that had any privacy. I wasn't going to take him to the tiny box Oberon and I slept in—and did more than sleep. No way.

I was relieved when Chloe led us to a tiny meeting room —four chairs bolted to the floor, no table, a vid screen on one wall, and literally nothing else.

"You okay?" She looked at me to let me know I didn't have to be in here, talking to Zarren, if I didn't want to. She had my back. Which I appreciated. But if there was one thing I was certain of, it was that Zarren would never physically harm me. Never.

Break my heart? Well, he'd already done that.

"I'm good. It's okay."

Chloe nodded and closed the door. I didn't realize how nervous I was until my entire body jumped at the sound of the door locking into place.

I expected Zarren to start talking right away, scream at me for taking his prisoner and leaving his ship, yell at me for breaking our match and so obviously being intimate with Oberon, demand I never touch Oberon again, try to convince me to give him another chance, tell me anything and everything I wanted to hear to win me back.

He did none of those things.

He didn't make a sound, simply closed the distance between us and pulled me into his arms. He held me. Close. Stroked my back. My hair. He said nothing for a long time, long enough that all the chaos and pain of the last few days welled up inside me and slipped from the corners of my eyes. Tears.

Why was I crying?

Because you still love him, woman. It's obvious.

I can't. It won't work.
And yet...

HE WAS HERE. So strong and mean and sure of himself. I considered pulling away, resisting, but he felt too damn good. Oberon adored me. He was fierce, and fun, and would never hurt me, never lie to me. He listened. He was honorable.

I loved so many things about Oberon. But he wasn't like *this*.

Unbreakable. Unyielding. So fucking strong. Mentally. Physically. Everything about Zarren made me feel invincible. Including his devotion to me. He had warned me he would not love me. I had told him I didn't need love.

What a little liar I turned out to be.

I clung, soaked him in. God, I'd missed him.

Why did he have to be so heartless? Why did he have to make the one decision I could never forgive? By leaving those women in prison cells, he left me there as well.

"Are you unharmed?"

"I'm fine." Technically true. Physically, at least. Mentally? I was confused. I was in love with two warriors who hated one another. And I couldn't shake the creepy feeling that something was wrong. Just... wrong. With the ship? With the mission? With my completely fucked up love life? Best two out of three?

Zarren pulled away and I looked up into his tormented green eyes. I'd never seen that look before. "Willow, my lady, I understand why you took Oberon from my ship."

"You do?"

He cupped the side of my face with his hand and stroked my cheek with his thumb. What was it with these guys? Did they have a top-secret, Willow Baylor operating manual somewhere? *'Cup Willow Baylor's face in your big, strong hands and she'll melt.'*

"Yes." His thumb paused and he tilted his head. "You should have talked to me, mate, before you left. But I understand why you did not. The fault is mine."

What?

"I should have held you in my arms and asked about your nightmares the very first night."

"I hid them from you. I took off my collar and—"

"You hid nothing. I knew the moment your nightmares began each night. I allowed you to believe you sneaked from our bed. I was a coward. I did not want anything to interfere with the dream I was living with you. I was selfish and weak. I should have insisted. I knew you were suffering, and I did nothing. I did not protect you by naming a second. I will never forgive myself for failing to care for you as I should."

He stepped back and looked me over from head to toe, one fingertip lifted to trace the insignia on my uniform. I'd looked around, no one else on board the ship had one like mine.

"Prime Nial has marked you with full council protection. He gave you unrestricted access to the S-Gen machines, weaponry, comm blackouts, transport beacons. Why would he do that?" Zarren lowered his hand. "It appears, my lady, I did not know you at all."

Oh, but he did. I'd thrown myself into that match with everything in me. The mating collars had to have been turned up to maximum volume with all the emotions I'd thrown his way. I didn't hide or pretend when I was with him. I was myself.

Mostly. The most myself I'd been since I'd left Earth.

I looked down at my uniform and boots and thought

back to the blue dress I'd worn when I first met him. I'd loved that dress. "I was a law enforcement officer, back on Earth. I just... I didn't let that part of myself out." I sighed. "Actually, this change is your fault."

"How so?"

No lies between us, at least not from me. "Because being with you made me feel strong again. I had forgotten what that felt like, not being afraid all the time."

"No one will ever hurt you again, Willow. I swear it." The softness I'd sensed from him vanished in an instant. "Why did you not tell me about your time with the Hive?"

I shrugged. "You didn't ask, and I don't like talking about it."

"Did you tell him?"

Him being Oberon. Here we go. "Yes."

"Why?"

"I don't know." I really didn't. Because he was safe? Kind? Because he held me in his arms after one of my nightmares and dared to ask? Or because I was finally ready?

"Because you believe his sister is their prisoner?"

"Isn't she? Isn't that why we're all here?" It was my turn to step back as rage bubbled up and filled me to the breaking point. "Oberon told you his sister was a prisoner on that base. And you were going to blow it up anyway? Kill her and all the other prisoners? Women like me? That could have been me. You don't know. That could have been me!"

Zarren moved forward to take me into his arms once more. I stepped back and pushed his hand out of the way.

"No. Don't touch me. I can't believe you. I can't. How could you?"

Rather than push me any further than he already had, he sat down in one of the chairs and waited for my blood pressure to come back down.

"The day I discovered Amalia Arcas had gone missing, I sent out an order to gather all relevant information. There were others taken, Willow, at least a dozen more from Prillon Prime alone. My people compiled a list. Names. Faces. Personal items, if we could acquire them without upsetting the families. Once I had enough information, I sent out a team of Elite Hunters. Not just Kayn—who is the best I've ever seen—but several others as well. I do not know what you may have learned about the Everians, but they can track anyone, anywhere, across galaxies. Their Elite Hunters' abilities are well known and have been tested, and found to be true, over and over, for thousands of years."

"So? What does this have to do with Oberon? Or you and that stupid doctor melting his skin off?" I didn't care what Oberon said about them being weak. Torture was torture.

"Kayn and the others searched for three weeks. They found nothing, love. No trail. No hint of the missing females' energies. Nothing."

"I don't understand. Why are you telling me this?"

"There is only one thing a Hunter cannot find. One type of individual capable of evading them. One, Willow. Only one."

"What? A Hive Soldier? An animal?"

"A corpse."

Oh, shit. "Doesn't Oberon know this, too? About the Hunters?"

"Of course."

"Then, I don't understand. Are you telling me that you told him that you had *proof*? From an Everian Hunter? And he still didn't believe you?"

"Yes, that is exactly what I am telling you." He moved as

if to stand, but I held my hand in front of me, palm out, to stop him. He settled in his seat.

"You told Oberon the Hunters couldn't find any trace of her? And you are sure, one hundred percent sure, that means she's dead? Without doubt? Dead?"

"Yes. I am sorry. Believe what you will about me. She, and the others, are gone. I would not leave females to suffer at the hands of those monsters, Willow. Neither will I order good warriors to their deaths in an attempt to save prisoners who cannot be saved. I will not sacrifice the living for the dead, simply because one stubborn Prillon male refuses to accept the truth. I am an honorable male."

"Then, why are we all here? Why did Prime Nial send all these people to help attack the Hive base?"

His sigh was deep. Tired. "Because Thomar Arcas sits on his war council. Because Bastion Arcas was fundamental in your rescue from the Hive prison ship. Because I did not inform Prime Nial, or the war council, of the base's existence, nor about the failed hunt for Amalia and the others. I gain knowledge and make decisions on my own, perhaps far too often. I did not wish to burden them with something they could not change when I knew, beyond all doubt, Amalia is not a prisoner on that base."

"Why were you melting his skin off?"

"He would not reveal the base's location. It needs to be destroyed. A Hive facility of that size can wipe out an entire planet's population in a matter of weeks. I could not take that risk."

"But you were going to blow up the base, without even checking? What if there are other prisoners there?" Other females, maybe not Amalia, maybe humans? *Like me.*

"My love, what if a hundred warriors die trying to get inside, and we find nothing?" This time he did stand, but I backed away, moving toward the door as he kept talking. "What if we do not destroy the base and the Hive use that facility to invade and capture innocent civilians, take over an entire planet or star system? Annihilate billions?"

This was not happening. I couldn't—no. Just no. Everything was wrong.

I moved close enough to activate the door's sensor. The panel slid open so I could make my escape. I needed time to process all of this. I needed to *think*.

I didn't move fast enough. Before I could leave, Zarren stood before me. He didn't block the exit, that would have just infuriated me. Worse, he stood to the side and waited for me to choose. Stay. Go. Believe him, or not.

Was Oberon so stubborn, so blindly devoted to his family, to his sister, that he would ignore Zarren's warning and charge into that Hive deathtrap just to see the truth for himself? Was he willing to get all of these people killed because he refused to believe the word of an Elite Hunter? Not just any Hunter. Kayn.

Was he willing to risk entire planets full of people on the off chance the Hunters were wrong, and his sister was still alive? And even if she was alive, and the Atlans he'd been working with were right, and she *was* on that base, was her life worth more than the billions of people Zarren was supposed to protect?

Was one life worth the lives of all the people on this ship?

Would mine have been? If I'd been asked? What would I have said when I was lying, cold and naked, in that cell? When Nexus 5 taunted and tortured me?

I'd spent over ten years of my life as a police officer. Protect and serve. That's what I tried to do. How was this any different? What was one life worth?

What was *my life* worth?

"Willow, please. I lied to you. I told you I would never love you. I was a fool. I have loved you from the moment I saw you. I love you still."

I wanted to believe him, so badly, my longing like a fist trying to yank my heart out of my chest while it was still beating. It *hurt.*

He leaned down. I knew what he was going to do. Kiss me. Kiss me and make me remember how much I loved him. How badly I'd wanted to believe in our happily-ever-after.

His lips met mine. His arms wrapped around my body. I melted. This was Zarren. My mate. He was supposed to be mine. I was supposed to be happy.

A bellow of rage crashed through my sensual haze. Zarren was yanked from my arms, his body thrown down the corridor by an enraged Prillon warrior.

Oberon.

"You fucking bastard. Don't fucking touch her."

Zarren rose from where he'd skidded into the hard metal wall. "She is my mate, Arcas."

A crowd gathered, every damn person on the ship appeared to be shoving closer to watch my life disintegrate before my very eyes.

"My collar is around her neck, Helion. She rejected your match. You hurt her. You lost her. She's mine. There's not one fucking thing you can do about it."

Zarren's eyes changed, became dark. Cold.

Deadly.

18

Oberon

He kissed her.

She kissed him back.

Fuck.

I stared into the eyes of a Prillon warrior who would fight to the death for the one and only thing that mattered to him, his mate.

Helion had to be looking into a fucking mirror because I felt the exact same way. Willow was mine. He had his chance with her. He fucked it up.

She was in my bed last night. In my arms. My cock brought her pleasure. My seed filled her pussy, marked her with my scent. My collar was around her neck—an Arcas family collar. She was under my protection, by law and by my choice.

"Go back to your ship, Helion. Leave her alone. Don't make me kill you."

"Go ahead. Try."

"Stop it! Both of you! This is stupid!" Willow's cries fell on deaf ears, mine and Helion's. There was no stopping this. A mate was sacred. Untouchable.

He'd fucking touched her.

I launched a series of punches, head, throat, body. I hit hard and fast.

He blocked every move and countered.

We broke apart, circling, both bleeding.

He wasn't bleeding enough.

"Stop!"

Helion charged this time, his kick knocked my feet out from under me, but I managed to pull him down with me.

"Shit. Get me out of here. I can't watch this."

I heard her, noted that Rukzi escorted her from the room.

Good. He was worthy. He could protect my mate while I finished killing this fucking bastard.

Helion managed to reverse, using my momentum against me until he had me pinned to the floor. I lifted one leg and wrapped it around his neck, flipped him. Locked my arm around his neck. I'd fucking choke him to death if I had to.

He flipped up, over my head and out of my hold. Suddenly he was behind me, his arm around my throat.

I threw an elbow to his face. Heard the bones in his nose break. Hit him again, harder.

An ion blast hit me in the side.

A second hit Helion.

"You two knock this shit off right now or I'll throw you both out an airlock." Commander Phan stood off to the side, blaster pointed right at us.

Neither one of us moved.

"God damn it." She fired again. Twice.

The blast burned, lit the nerves on my entire side on fire. Broke a rib.

Maybe Helion was responsible for the rib.

"Enough, Chloe. Enough." Helion groaned as he released me. We both rolled away from one another. Helion's mouth and neck were soaked in blood. Fuck yes, broke that bastard's nose.

My vision blurred. What the fuck?

I reached up to feel my forehead. Wet. I looked at my fingers. Coated with blood. When had that happened? Maybe that's why my head felt like it was about to explode.

I pulled myself to my feet, disappointed to discover Helion had done the same.

Our gazes locked.

"Oh no you don't." Chloe stepped between us. "Don't start that shit on my ship."

"Apologies, Commander." Not for making Helion bleed, but for making a mess on her ship.

"Save it." She ran a hand through her hair and shook her head. Again. "You two have a problem."

Helion didn't speak, just glared at me.

I glared back.

"You two have a huge problem. Willow loves you, both of you. So, you better fucking figure out how to get along."

"No." Helion's response was also mine.

No fucking way. She confided in me. Trusted me. Gave herself to me. *Wanted* me. The moment this mission was over I would claim her, name a second, and make sure she never had to see Helion's arrogant face again.

This cold-hearted bastard would never touch her. *Hurt* her.

Make her fucking cry. I could kill him for that alone.

She'd been through enough. So much. He had no idea how strong she was. How incredible.

How fragile. She was just beginning to reach out, take chances, *live*. She was vulnerable right now. Barely getting her feet back under her, feeling confident.

I wasn't about to allow Helion to fuck that up.

"Willow deserves better than you." I dared Helion to deny the truth.

"I agree. But I'm not letting her go."

"You don't have a choice."

This time it was Captain Mills, Chloe's mate, who stepped between us. "All right, assholes. Knock it off and get to medical. We have an op to run."

Willow

THANK god Chloe let me sit next to her in the control room. She had full access to everyone's helmet vids, vitals, and comms as we watched the ReCon team move closer to the Hive base's entrance.

That was her mate down there. How did she stand it?

Oberon was on the Atlans' stolen Hive ship, flying straight into the heart of the base like they belonged.

Zarren's focus was complete, over on his side of the small operations room. He was monitoring everything. Both teams. This ship. His ship. All communications, drone positions, and scanning for enemy combatants. He was the puppet master, watching the drama unfold on the stage below. Making minute adjustments. Noticing things no one else did.

"ReCon, hold your position. Drone will be clear in sixty seconds."

"Roger that. Sixty seconds." Captain Mills responded. I knew because I saw the comm indicator on his data screen light up.

I looked at Chloe, who appeared to be calm, cool, and collected.

Life goals.

"I thought there were a lot more drones." Based on the plans I'd seen them argue over for the last few hours, the place had been crawling with them, literally, everywhere, like ants protecting their anthill.

"There were."

"Where did they all go?"

"Excellent question." Zarren sounded suspicious.

I still felt like something was wrong. Nothing I could explain, just a cold knowing that wouldn't go away.

Since I had no idea what I was going to do about my two Prillon warriors, Oberon insisted they check the base for survivors—even if his sister wasn't among them—and Zarren frowned at everyone, told them it was a bad idea, and agreed to help anyway. Well, how the hell was I supposed to feel about all that? Warm and fuzzy?

I knew Zarren was doing this for me. Only for me. Because he'd told me.

Oberon was flying into my worst nightmare, hoping against all odds that he'd find Amalia there, alive, and somehow manage to get her out.

The Atlans were out for blood. Only their need for payback was eclipsed by the Hyperion's. Rukzi had gone full claw, still no clothes, and been first onto the invading ship.

They were all out of their god damn minds.

At least Zarren and Oberon hadn't tried to kill each

other again. Yet. I didn't know what was going to happen once the mission was over. No matter which one I chose, I'd be leaving half of my heart behind.

How the hell had I managed to screw things up this badly?

It's a gift, that's for sure.

Now is not the time, woman.

Now is all you've got. They're not going to give you a lot of time to think it over.

I know.

"We're in. Level five. Corridor clear." Seth again.

Chloe activated her comm. "Remember, if you find a Nexus unit, we need him alive."

"Worried I'll get trigger happy?"

Her grin told me he wasn't only talking about the mission.

"The ship is inside. On the ground." Zarren informed Chloe and the ReCon team. I glanced over my shoulder at his vid screens and watched Rukzi jump out of the ship and land in a crouch. He was moving forward, out of sight before the first Atlan had his boots on the ground. "Ruk, get your ass back with the others."

"You do not command me, Prillon."

"Fuck. I knew he was going to be a problem." Zarren rubbed his brow but ignored the Hyperion and his bad attitude.

I kinda liked the guy. When I'd needed to get away from the fight, he'd been the one who noticed I was about to lose my shit. He'd picked me up and carried me to transport, taken us both back to the Atlans' ship, and started pouring the wine.

Yes, definitely liked that one. Didn't like the headache that seemed to be coming on like a freight train. Should have made sure to drink more water. Or stick one of their ReGen wands in my pocket.

Maybe I'd ask the S-Gen machine for one later. Right now, headache or not, I wasn't leaving this room.

Oberon was down there. So was everyone else, but he was mine.

As much as Zarren was mine. Which was, technically, not at all.

"Level five clear. Moving to level four."

"Keep your eyes open, I can't scan that deep underground." Zarren warned them and moved on. "Enzo, what's your status?"

I stood up and moved to a seat closer to Zarren. He had monitors from every Atlan's, Oberon's and Bastion's helmets, each perspective displayed on a separate screen.

I watched until someone looked at Oberon. He was safe. Unhurt. Moving.

I could breathe.

"This isn't right." Zarren voiced what I'd been feeling for hours. He activated his comm. "Enzo, Arcas, fall back."

"Negative. Moving forward to the prison level." Enzo's voice came through clearly. He wasn't leaving until they'd seen the prison cells for themselves.

"Fuck."

Knowing their past as prisoners themselves, I understood. I reached out and put my hand on Zarren's shoulder. The tension coming off him was so strong, I didn't need a mating collar to feel his concern. "They need to see for themselves."

"I don't like it. There should be Hive Soldiers everywhere. Three Scouts on every entrance. Ten times this many drones." He tapped his fingertips on his control panel. "They're going to get themselves killed."

Sacrifice the living for the dead?

I hoped not.

"Level four clear. No hostiles. I think they abandoned the base." Seth and his ReCon team were moving through the outer sections, top to bottom, while Oberon and the Atlans worked from the inside, lower levels, moving up.

Theoretically, they would meet on the middle, grab any prisoners, and get the hell out of there.

Rukzi, who had reluctantly agreed to wear a small comm implant behind his ear, growled to the teams. "The human is right. I do not smell any recent life forms. They are not here. Their scent is several hours old."

"Then where the fuck are they?" Zarren squinted at his screen, flipped through several others until he landed on the map of the base. The drawings that had started this whole thing.

I didn't bother to study the layout. I was relieved no one was going to get hurt or killed.

I listened as the two teams cleared floor after floor, area after area. No resistance. No Hive at all.

After what felt like forever, Enzo said what I'd both hoped, and dreaded, hearing.

"Prison cells empty. Personal items remain. Female. Any prisoners they had are gone now."

Oberon launched into a litany of curses, some of them Prillon words I'd never heard before. And I thought I'd heard them all.

He was hurting. Amalia wasn't there. No one was there.

Chloe sighed. "You know the drill. Lab records. Operational reports. Anything you can find, I want it."

"Yes, ma'am."

I couldn't hear any longer. My head was pounding, and my nerves were shot. "I need to go lay down."

Chloe didn't even look up at me. "Headache?"

"Migraine."

"Stress will do that. Go ahead. I'll let you know if anything exciting happens."

Code for she'd let me know if anything happened to Oberon.

I shuffled out of the small room with everything spinning. I had my eyes closed, or as near as I could make them, and used my hand on the wall as a guide. Light hurt. Sound hurt. This sucked. No more wine for me.

Never was a big drinker. Should have known better.

Says everyone with a hangover, ever.

Shut up.

"Willow? Do you need help? I can escort you to your room."

Zarren. Would it be nice if he just carried me? Sure. But I wasn't ready for that. For him. Not yet.

"No. I'm going to medical to grab a ReGen wand. I'll be fine."

"Very well." I knew him, knew that tone. He was disappointed. With me.

I took three more steps when I felt it.

Energy, raw energy. Like a transport pad.

I looked up, forced my eyes to open, my brain to process what I was seeing.

Nexus 5 stood so close I could smell him. Dark blue skin, eyes dead and black. So tall, like Rukzi. Too big to fight.

I'd tried. So many times.

"Willow. My Willow. Bends, yet never breaks. I knew you would come back to me."

Oh, fuck me! I remembered that voice. Had nightmares about it.

Zarren yelled.

Nexus 5 grabbed me, his arms like steel bands. Unbreakable.

The air crackled and burned, ice cold.

Nexus 5 held me pressed to his body. Energy rose like a wave around us.

Transport. He was taking me off the ship.

I was his prisoner.

Again.

19

Zarren Helion

Shock. Horror. Rage. Terror.

I put it all away and activated my comm. "Kayn, Raz, get the fuck over here. I need you. Now!"

Chloe was watching me, waiting. "What happened?"

"A Nexus unit grabbed Willow and transported her off the ship."

"Oh, god." My infallible commander turned pale and grabbed onto the doorframe for support.

"Who is the best pilot here?"

"You know who."

"Oberon."

Her nod confirmed it. Fuck.

Didn't matter. If he was the best, he was fucking coming. "Get him. Now."

"On it."

I took two steps and turned back. "How did that thing get through our shields?"

"I don't know."

"That's a problem." I looked around at the perfectly good ship. It might as well be a scrap heap if we couldn't keep the Hive from transporting in on top of us. "Initiate Protocol Nine."

And I thought Chloe couldn't get any paler.

"Nine. Are you sure?"

"Do it. And get my ship into position."

"Yes, sir." She turned around and went back to her comm station. I didn't wait to hear what she said to Oberon. Didn't fucking care. The only thing that mattered was going after Willow as quickly as possible.

I activated my personal comm, ready to tell Oberon to get his ass moving. Chaos erupted. Too many voices, all shouting.

"It's an ambush."

"Fuck!"

"Behind you—"

"Down! Get down!"

Rukzi roared, in a killing rage.

Bedlam. I couldn't untangle one Atlan's voice from another. Chloe's calm orders fell over the top of them like water putting out a fire.

"Retreat to level four. Elevators there will take you to high ground. There's a perch. You can pick them off from there."

"Moving. Move! Move! You heard her!"

"Oberon, transport to the ship immediately."

"I can't leave them, there's too many. What the fuck—"

"Willow's been taken," I interrupted whatever heroic, save-my-friends babble was about to come out of his honorable, self-righteous, warrior's mouth. "So shut the fuck up and transport. I need a pilot."

He didn't want to leave in the middle of the fight? I didn't fucking care. The warriors on that base were tough. Experienced. Killers. Every fucking one.

Willow was not.

My Willow. Bends, but never breaks...

I was going to break every bone he had, tear that blue fucker's head off his neck and shove it down his throat. Gut him.

The Nexus unit knew her. Wanted *her*. Alive.

He wouldn't kill her. At least, not soon.

No, he wanted to have some fun with her first.

Oberon

I stared at the Elite Hunter sitting in the co-pilot's seat.

What the fuck was taking so long?

Willow had been gone for over an hour.

Sixty fucking minutes with that *thing,* the creature who had tortured her, taunted her, frozen her half to death and starved her until she was so weak, she couldn't stand. Experimented with her body and her mind. Pushed her to the breaking point. Nearly killed her half a dozen times.

Every word Willow had whispered to me in the dark became a living, breathing nightmare in my mind.

The ship was small, built for one-on-one combat. It was also the fastest thing in the Fleet. Every seat in the tiny cockpit was occupied. Me. Helion, looking as sick as I felt. The warlord from Helion's ship, Razmus. And Kayn. The Elite Hunter who had insisted my sister was dead.

Right now, I hoped he was every bit as good as Helion claimed.

Kayn's hands roamed over a star chart on his navigation panel, his gaze darting from one star to the next, moving on.

"Here." He pointed to a nearby star system.

I pulled up the data and frowned. The red dwarf was surrounded by at least fifteen inhospitable planets. Twice that many moons. Nothing lived in that system. Nothing could survive there. The Fleet didn't bother mining, too much effort when the raw materials were more readily available in hundreds of other systems.

"Why would he take her there?"

"Shut the fuck up and go where he tells you. He's not wrong."

I glared at Helion, who was in the seat behind Kayn's. I pulled up my own navigational chart and pointed to the place we'd lost the trail. "If he continued on this course, he'd be on the opposite side. Here."

"A ruse. He is there." Kayn pointed to the same system he had before, at the piles of dust and death that barely passed for planets.

"Do as he says, Arcas. Every moment we delay is another he is alone with her." Exactly. Helion didn't need to remind me. I knew. I fucking knew, and it was making me sick. How the fuck was he so calm?

"This doesn't make sense. His ship has not altered course since we found his trail. Why would he make a hard right into a place like that?"

"Trust me." Kayn's gaze locked with mine. "Trust me. I can feel him. He is there."

"You willing to bet her life on that? And yours? Because I'll kill you if you're wrong."

"Yes." The Hunter faced forward as I entered the coordinates into the ship's system. "And you are welcome to try."

I didn't care enough to argue. We were both covered in Hive blood, both exhausted.

I pushed the fighter hard and fast, scanning just far enough ahead to keep us from flying nose first into an asteroid or floating debris. I hoped.

"Commander, this is Enzo. Please respond."

Helion flipped on the comm next to his head. "This is Helion."

"The base has been cleared."

"Casualties?"

"Three. All ReCon."

"Captain Mills?"

"Negative. He made it. He's in medical. Nothing that won't heal."

Three dead, my fault. My fucking fault. Helion told me my sister wasn't on that base. I should have listened.

"Is Captain Arcas with you?" Enzo asked.

"I'm here." Why did he want to talk to me?

"Our system has been scanning the data we recovered from the lab."

Everything inside me went still as I waited. A new voice came over the comm.

"Oberon, it's Bastion. Amalia was here. She's listed in their fucking reports." His voice cracked and I knew.

I *knew*.

"She died the second day. They were apparently exposing the females to different atmospheric gases, and she didn't make it. None of them did. Seventeen females, fourteen Prillon, two Atlans, and one hybrid from Rogue 5."

"Fuck!" I slammed my hand down on the ship's control panel and shuddered. She was dead. Had been dead for months. I'd been afraid to face the truth, too fucking stubborn to let go.

Pain sliced through me, but it was not as sharp as it should have been. I'd been chasing a dream, a fool's hope. I'd been lying to myself, but part of me knew the truth.

Elite Hunters were never wrong.

Two days? Those fuckers had killed her in two days?

Willow had been in that lab for two years.

Two fucking years.

"I'm sorry." Kayn looked at me. There was no judgment in his eyes. "I hate knowing. I hate telling family members even more."

"Fuck." I looked back at Helion, who remained silent. He was right. He'd been right the entire time. "I should have helped you blow that fucking base into dust."

"Perhaps. And perhaps we will acquire information stored in their systems that leads us to a major victory."

What the fuck did he just say to me? Was he trying to appease me? Erase my guilt?

"I was wrong, Helion. Three members of Captain Mills' ReCon team are dead, and the Nexus unit has Willow."

"You were wrong. You refused to give up. You loved her."

Fuck yes. I did. I'd held her in my lap when she was barely knee high and told her stories. I'd scared off young warriors who took note of her beauty. I'd danced with her on her birthday and laughed when she stepped on my toes. When she'd been scared because I joined the Coalition Fleet, I promised her I would live forever.

I expected to die. I accepted the risk.

I'd gone to war. She was supposed to be at home, safe.

Why wasn't she there, in mother's garden, giggling with her friends and gossiping about warriors?

Why the fuck did I leave her unprotected?

"Oberon. Focus. You lost one female you love. If we don't track down that Nexus, we're going to lose another." Helion's gaze locked onto mine and held. "Get me there, Arcas. Fucking get me there."

I'd been mistaken. It wasn't calm I saw behind his eyes; it was death.

20

Willow

I EXPECTED to wake up and be right back where I started; naked, cold, lying on the floor with an energy barrier trapping me inside a cell not much bigger than a large bathtub.

Instead, I was on a bed. The blanket under my cheek was soft and warm.

I wiggled my toes. No boots, but my uniform was still in place. I wasn't naked.

Headache reduced to a dull roar.

Had it all been a nightmare? Was seeing Nexus 5 just a bad dream? I'd dreamed of Nexus 5 so often, especially in the months immediately following my rescue, that for a time I'd had to fight to determine what was real and what was not.

I rolled over and blinked a few times to clear my vision. The bed I was on was big enough for several people. I was like a single pea in the center of a large pod. Everything was blue, shades of blue. The bedding, the walls, the soft rugs spread along the floor.

The alien leaning forward, elbows on his knees, watching me.

Oh, shit.

I told you to stop saying that.

Nexus 5 actually smiled, or what passed for a smile with him. "I had forgotten what a pleasure you are to listen to, arguing with yourself."

Something I could only describe as a shadow moved through my mind, touching here and there, like a slight, cool breeze.

It was *him.* Inside my head. Just like before.

"Yes, my Willow, I am with you. Inside you. I ached when you left me, mate. Why would you do such a thing?"

Mate? Did he just call me his fucking mate? No. Never. I'd die first.

"I believed you might feel that way. But I spent the time without you answering a very important question. Why did you leave me? You were strong, my Willow, stronger than all the others. Worthy. Able to carry the seeds of our people."

"You are not my people."

"Am I not?" He stood slowly and I sat up in turn, keeping pace as he rose to his full height and held out his arms for inspection. He moved his fingers, five of them, on a hand that, other than being three different shades of blue and tough as old cow leather, looked remarkably human.

But he had claws, like Ruk did. I'd seen them...

He walked on two legs, not tentacles or insect-like appendages that could twist this way and that.

His chest was wide. Shoulders strong. His face—if one could get past the dead, black eyes—no, not dead, deep. His face was not unpleasant to look upon...

He's playing you. Pay attention.

"Stop. I can feel you in my head, influencing my thoughts. I don't want you. I don't want to be with you. I don't want to touch you."

I sure as hell didn't want *him* to touch *me*.

I scrambled off the side of the bed, as far away from him as I could get. Glanced down. Shit, my boots were on the other side, next to him.

Not that it mattered. Boots were the least of my worries. I'd played this cat and mouse game with him before.

I always win. His smug response played in my head like a broken record.

Was that what he wanted here? To win? Win what?

"You are my mate, Willow. You will stay here, with me. I will fuck you, as I have seen the others do, in your memories. You will bear my children."

"No." Never. He'd never tried anything like this before.

I had to get the hell out of here. Wait!

I patted the pocket that held my—

"Looking for this, my Willow?" Nexus 5 held my transport beacon in one hand. He tilted his head to watch me as he wrapped his hand in a fist around it. He made no expression, no other movement, as he crushed the technology in his hand. He rubbed his fingers across his palm and lowered his gaze as we both watched slivers and dust float to the floor.

Shit.

Now what?

What would Zarren do, if he was here, in a body my size? With no boots?

I got nothing.
Well, think of something.
You first.

He will come for me. Both of them will come.

Nexus 5 drifted across my thoughts like a shadow, his presence a chill I recognized...

"Oh, god." I wrapped my arms around my waist and stared. "It was you. I was feeling you." The unease and anxiety. Nerves, I'd thought. The feeling of dread. Fear. The headache. Not wine induced. *Him.* All of it because this *thing* had been in my head.

"I have a name, mate. Although, if you prefer to call me a more human title, I will allow it."

How about asshole?

Are you trying to get us killed?

Nexus 5 chuckled again, his laughter one of the strangest things I'd ever heard. "I was thinking, perhaps Phillip?"

"That's my father's name." What the hell? Did he want me to call him *Daddy?* Because that was not fucking happening.

"The name of a male you cared for and trusted. Someone you loved."

"He's dead."

"Very well." I felt him move around inside my head, searching. "Joseph?"

A fellow officer. A friend from long ago. "No. Why are you doing this? You know I will never agree. I will never stop trying to get away from you."

He turned and walked away from me, toward what I realized was a blank monitor of some kind. He waved his hand and the screen filled with images I recognized. The Hive base.

Enzo and Ruk's *ship.*

"I realized, over the weeks and months of searching for you, that I made an error in my dealings with you."

Ya think? An error? Was that what the Hive called torture these days?

"I allowed you to believe, my Willow, that there existed a world you desired to return to."

What?

"The moment I felt your presence, I knew this was my chance to correct that error."

"Felt my presence?"

"Of course. We are one, mate. Linked more closely than anything those Prillons and their pathetic collars could achieve."

Collar? I reached up to feel for Bastion's collar around my neck. It was gone.

I was not going to lose it in front of this *thing*. I lowered my hand and glared directly into his dark pits for eyes. "I will never choose you. Just let me go."

"Why would I do that? You will stay. You will accept me into your body, fuck me, as the other males say. You will be mine."

"No."

He twitched one finger and the image zoomed in close enough that I could see movement inside the base. Figures in uniforms. I watched as Enzo and his team—Oberon included—walked back up the ramp of their ship and then watched as the ship lifted off, leaving the base behind. It flew away, out into space, the base growing smaller behind it.

How did he have an image of it from this angle?

"Why are you showing me this?"

"Not all my drones are surveillance only, mate. How would I protect you, if that were the case?"

"I'm sure you have a hundred mindless Soldiers wandering around here."

"Forty. I do. Not mindless, mate. One mind. And a doctor, to care for you and ensure the safe birth of our first child."

Not happening.

No fucking way.

On that, old me and new me were in complete agreement.

"Do not interrupt. I am telling you a story, mate. Humans enjoys stories, do you not?"

Not touching that one.

He faced the screen again. Kept talking. Out loud. Which was weird. I was much more accustomed to hearing him inside my head.

Do you prefer this? A much more intimate form of communication I prefer as well.

No. Get out of my head.

"Very well. You see, I can be responsive to your needs."

When I didn't say—or *think*—anything, he continued. "I realized, mate, that you would not choose to stay unless there was nothing for you to return to."

What?

"When I sensed your presence in my mind, so close, I knew destiny had brought you back to me. Your arrival, and that of your friends, was welcome."

No.

"Your mind is even stronger now, my Willow. I slipped inside you slowly. Shared your pleasure with the other male. I knew, then, I had made a mistake with you. But you returned to me, and I had time to prepare, to ensure your previous attachments would no longer be a problem."

A dark pit opened up in my stomach as the ship on screen grew bigger and bigger.

"I know what you desire. How you want to experience

pleasure during mating. I will not fail this time. I cannot fail."

On the hunk of rock where the Hive built their base, an explosion filled the space behind Enzo's retreating ship. A flash of fire and light.

Before I could process what that would mean, a weapon of some kind appeared to come from behind the screen, from whatever place the camera was mounted, and enveloped Enzo's ship in a blast of light.

Another.

The ship exploded.

"*Oberon.*" His name was a whisper on my lips. I'd watched him get on that ship. Enzo. Ruk. All of them. Gone. "You fucking bastard!"

I charged him. I'd claw his eyes out of his hideous skull, rip those fucking *things* off the back of his head and watch him *bleed.*

He caught me with one huge hand wrapped around my throat. He lifted, just enough to force me onto my tiptoes. I had no leverage, no way to move. Or fight.

I kicked, but he was out of reach.

Damn it! No!

"I feel your grief, female. Yes. I planned well. But that male is not the only one you cared about."

The view on the screen changed to another ship. Black. Sleek.

"This ship brought you to me. The technology is interesting. I would not have discovered it, had you not been on board. I hate to destroy it."

"Liar." Now he was just toying with me.

"Indeed."

More bursts of light. The ship fired back at something, a buoy in space? A rock? I couldn't tell where the Hive's shots were coming from.

I clawed at the hands around my neck, sickly satisfied when I felt his flesh gather beneath my fingernails.

"This one, Zarren? He has been a problem for us for quite some time." Nexus 5 smiled, his pale, blue-white teeth hideous as he watched the ship catch on fire. "The others will celebrate with me, once he is gone."

Maybe they could get away. Go. Fly. Blast off.

The ship exploded.

No. No. No. No!

"I hate you."

Nexus 5 settled me back on my feet and released his hold on my neck. Oberon? Dead. Zarren? Dead. Chloe? Seth? Enzo? Ruk? Bastion? Dead, dead, dead. All dead.

I stumbled backward.

Nexus 5 walked to me and lifted one hand to my cheek. "You came back to me. I would not have known about the attack, would not have saved my Soldiers, if you had not been with me, part of me, in my mind."

I was the reason. For all of it. I stole Zarren's drawings and set Oberon free. I begged Danika for help, and Prime Nial sent an entire ReCon team. Bastion had come to us, to help look for Amalia. Who, according to Kayn and Zarren, was already fucking dead. The Atlans and Ruk? They would have attacked regardless, Oberon had told me that, but Nexus 5 wouldn't have *known they were coming.*

I'd killed them all. By being here. By failing to notice Nexus 5 was *in my head.*

The hand on my cheek barely registered. It didn't matter. Nothing mattered.

"Willow Baylor operating manual. My hand is on your cheek, mate. Should you not, as you put it, *melt?*"

I didn't think, I bolted, ran for the door. I expected it to be locked.

Instead, it slid open, revealing a corridor and two Hive Soldiers standing guard.

They were his, the other pieces of him. Closer to him than any of the others.

I recognized them both. They'd been with him *before*. For everything, watched everything that had been done to me.

One was Prillon. Golden skin and eyes. Silver integrations everywhere. The other looked like an oversized human, except for the fangs.

Fucking fangs.

God, I hated fangs.

Both stared at me, unmoved and unmoving, as I ran forward and lost my balance, scrambled on my hands and knees, regained my footing. I sprinted down the corridor, my bare feet slapping on the cold, hard surface. I risked a glance back over my shoulder.

The two guards had not changed position. Nexus 5 stood in the corridor, watching me.

There is nowhere to run, my Willow. I am inside you.

21

Willow

How long had I been hiding? An hour? A day? Time meant nothing. All I could think about was my mates. The explosions. Dead. They were dead.

My fault. They'd been like lambs to slaughter because I was here. Because this monster was inside me.

Stop running, female. I feel your hunger. You have a laceration on your foot.

What? Now he didn't want me half-starved and miserable? Bleeding? In pain? Why not? So he could get me pregnant?

God, no.

I crouched down behind a service duct and closed my eyes. I had deliberately wandered, not caring which direction I chose to go. Feeling my way along the wall whenever I was able. I didn't want him watching through my eyes. I didn't think more than two steps ahead because I didn't' want him to know where I was going.

His frustration was building. I could feel it.

I rested my arms on my knees and put my head down. There had to be a solution, a way out of this.

I couldn't stay here and become what he wanted to make me. He had a cock, I'd seen it before. Big. Blue.

Yeah, no. That thing's not getting anywhere near you.

No kidding.

You know what we have to do. There is only one way out of this.

I know.

I thought of Zarren, of our first night together. The way we'd both lost control when the collars connected us. So hot. His cock so deep inside me I never wanted to stop. My back against the wall as he thrust hard and fast. Over and over.

Cease these thoughts and come to me.

He was irritated now. Too bad. Because Oberon's mouth was bliss. He worked me into a frenzy, his hands everywhere. His tongue, inside me, his fingers, inside me. His cock, sliding deep as I came, my orgasm an explosion all over his hard length.

Willow, come to me. I will make you feel these things. They are gone. There is only me.

Over my dead body.

That's what I was saying, woman. You get one asshole's voice inside our head and you ignore me?

I heard you. But I can't leave him here. He'll just do this to someone else.

What can you do? You don't have a weapon. He's twice your size.

I know. Shut up and let me think.

I had to stop him, and I didn't need to survive doing it. He was right about one thing, there was nothing left for me to go back to. Nexus 5 had used me to destroy everyone I cared about.

I felt my way through the dark, my hand along the wall as I bought myself some time. Keep moving. Keep thinking.

Every sci-fi movie I'd seen—and there weren't that many, I was more of a historical kind of girl—had a powerful hero swoop in to save the day.

No one's coming. What do they do when they know they're going to die?

The answer came to me like an arrow through my skull. *Destroy the ship.*

What?

Nexus 5 stirred, his anger amusing. *Do not think such things, mate. I tire of your game.*

Maybe he could find me, maybe he could not. I wasn't sure. All the time I'd spent around him, I'd pulled away. Resisted.

What if I did the opposite?

Woman, this is a bad idea.

Shut up.

I stopped my slow amble through the dark and made my mind quiet. Still. Silent. When his mind moved, I focused on the way he felt. Cold. Slow moving, like a mud slide.

Rather than turn away, I let it flow over me. Around me.

Suddenly, I was there. Inside his head. Looking through his eyes. The connection flowing between him and all of the Hive Soldiers present was like crackling background noise, dozens of radios all tuned to different stations. If I focused on listening to one, I could ignore the others. Move on.

Nexus 5 was agitated all right. Confused. Why did the

human female never react in a predictable manner? How was he going to save his people if he failed? Again?

They were all failing. Dying.

I didn't *think*, more like I imagined that I knew how to destroy this place. Had set something irreversible in motion.

His thoughts snapped the idea and formed images. He envisioned me, standing in some sort of control room—

She'll never find it. She doesn't know where it is...

I pushed the thought out, away from myself, into the cold sludge and waited for him to find it.

He did. Once more images flashed through my mind. A tunnel. A door.

A hidden room...

Inside the room, large, glowing crystals. Magnetic pieces spinning, spinning, using the energy of the planet to power everything.

Energy...stored in the crystals.

Willow wouldn't know what to do. She is human. Helpless. She would never...

His mind filled in the gap in my thought. I watched. I retreated, lifting my mind from the heavy weight of his slowly, carefully. I thought nothing. Felt nothing.

Like him. I made sure I felt like him.

As free as I would ever be, I locked the information I needed inside the little box I'd created inside my mind. A box he couldn't open. The box was very small. Locked. The entire time I'd been a prisoner, he'd never discovered it.

You sure about this?

Yes.

I moved quickly, taking the layout of my prison from his mind.

Feels good to be mind raping that fucker for once.

She wasn't wrong. I felt powerful. Sure. This was what

Zarren would do, if he were here. This was what Oberon would do. This was what a warrior would do.

Willow, enough. Stop. Return to your room.

There was force behind Nexus 5's command. Perhaps, before I'd felt Zarren's strength in my mind, the mental push would have been enough to stop me. Perhaps I would have obeyed.

Now it was too late. I'd arrived. The hidden door's panel slid open and I stepped inside.

Willow!

I smiled. *You lose, fucking asshole. You. Fucking. Lose.*

I had no idea what would happen when I reached for the first crystal. Would it burn? Shock me? Would it be hot or cold to touch?

Didn't matter. I needed to toss at least half of them into the whirling mass of magnetic disks and coils, each one bigger than I was. They weren't attached to anything. It was like they were floating in mid-air. I wasn't a scientist. I had no clue how any of this shit worked.

But Nexus 5 knew, and I'd stolen the information right out of his ugly, blue head.

I yanked the first crystal out of its place in the grid—was that computer stuff inside actually cut into the crystal?—and threw it as hard as I could. A flash of light temporarily blinded me when it shattered.

Willow! No!

Lesson learned. Close the eyes or deal with big, dark, flash-blind floaters blocking my vision every time.

I tossed another. And another.

The disks wobbled, the sound created a strange thumping in the air. The shock waves pushed at my chest. The coils made noise as well, like tapping a champagne flute with a fork. Ringing.

Something was definitely happening.

When I knew I had dislocated enough crystals to wreck the joint, I took one more from its place in the neat, precisely spaced energy grid, and slammed it down on what looked like the only control panel in the room.

Lights danced. An alarm went off outside, in the corridor. The grid, the walls, everything began to smoke. Little fires ignited all over the walls.

Oh, yeah. That did it.

I went back out into the corridor and sat with my back against the wall. I leaned my head back and smiled. I had five minutes, left? Ten? No idea.

Well played, Willow.

Why thank you. I agree.

I kept myself company, tried to fill my mind with memories I would miss.

Helion's kiss. Oberon's smile. Feeling totally and completely loved. Not everyone could say they'd ever experienced what I had. I'd be with them soon.

I was taking that mother-fucker with me.

"Willow!" I turned my head to see Nexus 5, his two side-brains, and at least half of his forces, if he'd told me the truth about their number, filling the corridor. "What have you done?"

Self-destruct, asshole. Bet you didn't plan for that.

Zarren Helion

"Kayn! Where the fuck are you?"

Raz roared behind me, a Hive soldier's arm in one hand, leg in another. I didn't look down, didn't need to. I'd seen beasts in battle. They didn't sneak around, aim and shoot.

They tore their enemies in half.

Oberon fought on my left, his blaster in one hand, blade in the other. A trail of three already dead behind him.

The Hunter's voice called from ahead. Right side.

"Over here! She's this way!"

"About fucking time." Oberon slashed the throat of his enemy and joined me as I ran toward Kayn's voice.

Willow was on this base. It was small, but not small enough.

I didn't have time to search every corridor and every room. Gods fucking knew what that Nexus unit was doing to her right fucking now.

"Raz, guard the ship. We need to be able to get off this rock."

The beast grumbled and turned back the way we'd come. Moments later his battle roar assured me I'd made the right call.

Find Willow. Get her out of here. Two clear objectives. I'd been on operations exactly like this one. Many times.

Not once had my heart been lodged in my throat like it was now. My gut churned. I was so agitated my aim was shaky. I fucking missed my last mark and had to rip out his throat, up close and personal. Wanted to do so again. I didn't normally count my kills. This time the urge to keep score rode me hard. Six, so far. Three more than Oberon, one less than Raz. The blood coating my armor didn't appease me, it made me want to kill *more of them. All of them.*

Fuck.

"We'll find her. She's tough." Oberon had performed a fucking miracle getting us through the Hive's automated defense cannons and into their landing bay. I'd never seen anything like it. My stomach had yet to recover from the violent twist and turns. Oberon had earned his reputation as one of the best pilots in the Fleet. If I'd been in the pilot's seat, we wouldn't be standing here now, drenched in enemy blood.

We wouldn't have a chance to save Willow.

Oberon took aim, fired. A Hive Soldier dropped from his place along the railing on the floor above us. Big fucker. He landed with a loud thump a few steps away.

More Hive Soldiers moved into position, taking his place, firing down on us. They had the high ground. Not good.

However, Kayn was leading us down, not up. Deeper into the bowels of the base.

To what? Waste systems? Mining operations? A dungeon?

I'd fucking filet the bastard if he'd put Willow in a dungeon.

Who was I kidding, I was going to kill him regardless.

An alarm filled the space. Urgent. Loud.

The Hive above us turned as a group and disappeared from sight.

"Where the fuck are they going?" Oberon pulled his weapon back and watched them run.

"Move it!" Kayn yelled at us and disappeared inside a shadowed corridor.

I heard his voice before I saw him. Deep. Angry.

"Willow! What have you done?"

Kayn moved like a ghost, his knife blade slicing the neck of the nearest Soldier. The second.

As a group, their backs were turned, all of them focused on something in front of them.

Until now.

Like watching a row of machines, they turned as one and faced us.

I looked past them.

Willow. She sat on the floor, her back to the wall. Her head was tilted back as the Nexus unit loomed over her.

She smiled at him.

"Get down!" Oberon shouted and I dropped into a roll as a long blade sliced through the air where my head had been.

I came up on my feet, shoved a blade between the Soldier's ribs and lifted him off his feet. I lifted the blaster in my other hand to the soft space under his jaw and turned his head into liquid inside his helmet.

With a roar I barely recognized, I shoved the dead body off my blade and attacked the next. "Willow!"

"Zarren!"

I stabbed my blade into my opponent's eye socket. Twisted. Tossed him aside like forgotten garbage.

Willow. Mate.

Mine.

Willow

Oh my god. Zarren? And Oberon? Kayn?

They were dead. They were supposed to be dead.

They're going to be dead, if they don't get out of here before this place blows.

Oh, shit.

"Get out of here! Run!" I tried to stand, to warn them.

Nexus 5's hand gripped my throat. This time, when he

held me by the neck, my shoulders slip *up* the wall and my feet left the ground.

I kicked. Scratched. God damn it. His arm was twice the length of mine.

I twisted enough to see Zarren's face. His gaze traveled the length of my body, stopped on the hand wrapped around my neck.

I closed my eyes. I couldn't watch him suffer. Nexus 5's thoughts were clear as day to me now. He was going to snap my neck and use Zarren's rage against him. Exploit Zarren's one weakness.

Me.

You better do something. Quick. This place is going to blow.

I know.

An image formed in my mind.

Won't work. He's too big.

I didn't have any other choice.

I locked both hands around his forearm, braced my shoulders against the wall and swung both legs up…up…up, and locked them around his head.

I dug my toes into the grooves separating the strange tentacles that ran like ropes along his spine, from the base of his skull to halfway down his back. I dug in, deep. Pushed like I was trying to break out of an egg.

His flesh tore. He screamed and tossed me away from him.

I fell flat on my back. My head hit the floor. Hard. I rolled onto my side and shoved up onto my forearms.

Zarren? Where was Zarren?

"Helion!" Nexus 5 screamed his name.

I tried to make sense of what I saw.

Kayn. He flashed from place to place, his blade cutting, retreating before the Hive could react. Strike. Disappear.

Oberon was surrounded, using his blaster to hold three enemies at bay while he fought another with his knife.

Zarren...

My mate was unrecognizable, drenched in blood, head, armor, boots. A pile of dead lay in his wake. No color but dark red was visible everywhere on his body—except his eyes. Those bright green eyes focused on Nexus 5 from a blood drenched face. Unblinking. Deadly. Like a demon's.

I am a monster, Willow. Nothing less.

He'd warned me.

Nexus 5 and Zarren moved at the same time. Zarren charged. Dodged one strike. Was hit by another.

They moved so fast I couldn't keep up. Limbs tangled and twisted, angry snarls and grunts of pain.

Zarren had him down. Nexus 5 fell to one knee.

In a fit of rage Zarren grabbed him, one hand shoved into Nexus 5's mouth.

He screamed as he tore the blue male's head in half, split his jaw into pieces, tore until the tentacle-like strands separated from the base of his skull.

Zarren threw the top of my captor's head aside and dropped the very dead body at his feet.

Shocked, I stared.

"Willow?"

Zarren didn't move, as if he was afraid to touch me.

I scrambled to my feet and threw myself into his arms.

"Willow, I'm—"

"Shh. Shut up. I don't care. I love you. I don't care how many monsters you kill. Just run. We have to run. I set a self-destruct."

"How long do we have?"

"I don't know. I'm sorry. I didn't think—" I didn't finish the thought. The tightening of his arms told me what I needed to know. He knew I hadn't planned on getting out of here alive.

"Oberon?" Zarren shouted.

"Clear."

"Clear." Kayn answered before Zarren could ask.

I didn't look down as my mate cradled me to his chest and ran out of the corridor. I'd seen them all. Bodies. Mangled. Cut. Torn in pieces. These three males were responsible for all of it.

Thank god.

He ran, Oberon and Kayn easily keeping pace. There were no more Hive, at least none that tried to stop us. I caught glimpses of them along the route, more bodies. The stench of death and blood was so thick I didn't know if I'd ever stop smelling it.

The ship we boarded was the smallest I'd seen. Not much bigger than my mother's old minivan, if the old van had wings and ion cannons attached to the sides. Four seats. Oberon took the pilot's seat. Zarren held me on his lap.

We all looked like we'd been put through a meat grinder and soaked in a blood brine.

No one spoke until the ship left the landing bay.

Zarren's was stroking my hair with one hand. I leaned against him, my cheek on his chest. Bloody? Yeah. I didn't care.

"Did you mean what you said?"

"Yes. I love you."

An explosion sounded through the comms. Zarren's muscles tensed.

"Fuck. That was close." Raz's rumble was almost a chuckle.

"Too close" Kayn agreed.

"Status?" Zarren's tone was all business. We weren't safe. Not yet.

Oberon checked the sensors. "We're good." He glanced over his shoulder to where I rested in Zarren's lap. His golden eyes locked on mine. "Are you—"

I gave him a smile. It was weak, but it was real. "I'm okay."

He opened his mouth, as if he wanted to say more, but looked up at Zarren and chose not to.

"Get my ship on comms."

Kayn moved as ordered. Before long Chloe's voice filled the small space.

"Helion? Did you find her?"

"Yes. Did you get everyone out in time?"

Chloe chuckled. After the horror of the last few hours, the sound was... jarring. "Oh, yes. Your ship is packed about as tight as it gets, but everyone's accounted for."

I leaned back to look up at Zarren. "Nexus 5 showed me the base blowing up. And the ship. How are you not all dead?"

Chloe's voice was a bit too chipper. "Protocol Nine. The moment Nexus 5 broke our security systems, we knew we had to get everyone out of there."

"You knew it was a trap?"

"When he took you, I knew. Not before." Zarren looked away from me to stare at the back of Oberon's head. What was I missing?

"What about the base?"

"It has been destroyed."

"And the prisoners? Amalia?"

Oberon's shoulders tensed, but he answered my questions. "She's gone. Bastion found the report in their records."

Oh, no. "I'm so sorry."

The four males settled into a heavy silence, one I didn't feel like treading upon.

I didn't want to think about any of this right now. Them. Me. I loved them both. I did.

But Zarren was mine. Soul deep. Forever. Every cell in my body belonged to him.

If he still wanted me, after everything I'd done.

I'd used up my daily supply of courage.

I didn't ask.

22

Willow, Battleship Zeus, Three Days Later

I was miserable, pacing in my quarters. Zarren was coming back from Prillon Prime today. At least, that's what he'd told me. I'd barely seen him since our run-in with Nexus 5. I'd been interviewed, poked and prodded, spent some time in a ReGen pod—even though I told them I didn't need it. I'd been asked to draw everything I'd seen inside that base, especially the room with the spinning coils and crystals. Turns out none of the Coalition scientists had any idea what the Hive were using to power that base.

I did what I could to kill time. I kept moving. If I stopped, I missed them.

Prime Nial and the war council were, apparently, not at all happy about everything that had happened, or about Zarren keeping so many secrets.

Oberon had gone to the capital as well. Kayn. Chloe. Seth. The only friend I had on this massive battleship was Warlord Razmus, who never left my side. He slept in full battle armor right outside my bedroom door.

I told him to give me a little space.

Raz informed me Zarren had threatened him with death if he did.

I rarely left my personal quarters. If the interested looks from the unmated males wasn't deterrent enough, the whispers and wide eyes chased me away.

Turned out, Zarren Helion wasn't just a commander, he was infamous.

I ran my palms over the front of the green dress I wore. The color matched his eyes. The gold thread? For Oberon's. Hidden, but there.

I had to tell him, when he returned. I loved him, but I couldn't be with him, not if it meant giving up Zarren.

A knock brought me to my feet.

Raz moved before I could. "Allow me, my lady."

I grinned. Like I had a choice in the matter. After the week I'd had, I didn't mind the extra protection, but I still had a blaster strapped to my thigh, under my skirt.

I waited for Raz to return.

Zarren appeared instead.

I didn't think, I ran for him. Leaped into his arms, sure he would catch me.

He held me. I breathed him in. "You're back."

"Did you miss me?" Was that teasing tone coming from *my commander?*

"Yes." I didn't feel like teasing. Not when I missed him so much it hurt.

He set me on my feet well before I was ready to let go. Which would be never.

"My lady."

I took a step back. That tone. Why? What was he about to tell me? What was wrong?

He dropped to one knee before me and held out his hand.

Three mating collars rested in his palm.

"Willow Baylor of Earth, I love you with everything I am, every part of me. Heart. Mind. Soul. I am yours. My body is yours. I wish to claim you as my mate. Will you accept my claim? Will you give yourself to me and my second freely, or do you wish to choose another primary male?"

The formal words, modified from the official Prillon mating ritual, wrecked me.

"Yes. I love you. I love you, so much."

I expected him to stand, but he did not. "I am a monster, Willow. You have seen the truth, watched me kill. Are you sure? Because if you say yes, I will never let you go."

"You are not a monster. You are brave and strong and exactly what I need."

He shuddered and closed his eyes, leaned forward to press his forehead to my abdomen like he was at prayer. I stroked his hair and waited for him to lift his face and look up at me. "Willow. I am yours."

"I love you. Every part of you. But I don't understand. You don't have a second."

He stood and reached for me. Before I knew it, I had a mating collar around my neck. His collar, back where it should be.

I reached for him, pulled his head down so I could kiss him. And kiss him.

With a chuckle—and a hard cock, yes, I'm naughty, I looked—he pulled away and took my hand. "My lady, my love, I would like you to meet your second, should you approve."

I turned, every part of me sparkling with hope.

Oberon.

Please, please, be Oberon.

A warrior emerged from the entrance. Tall. Strong. Handsome. Brown skin, rich brown hair. Golden eyes.

Mine.

"Oberon."

He stepped forward and knelt before me as Zarren had. "I pledged my life to you once. I do so again, and ask if you will accept me as your second mate. I vow to love you, protect you, and care for you in all ways until my dying breath."

"I love you." I leaned over, barely—even kneeling, these warriors were almost as tall as I was—and kissed him. I stood up and reached for Zarren. Pulled his lips to mine. "You two are sure about this? Last I checked, you hated each other."

"Hate is a strong emotion, mate." Zarren studied Oberon for a moment. "More like, frustration."

Oberon grinned. "Don't let him fool you. He admires everything about me."

Zarren frowned. "That may, perhaps, be true."

I took Oberon's hand and tugged to make sure I had his attention. "He tortured you."

"I was being foolish. And I told you, love, his methods were weak."

"Weak?" Zarren sounded outraged at the mere suggestion.

Oberon grabbed one of the two collars from Zarren's hand and lifted it to his neck. "We'd better do this before we change our minds."

Zarren lifted his own collar. "Indeed."

I held my breath, waiting to *feel* e-v-e-r-y-t-h-i-n-g.

My mates lowered their hands. I watched their collars resize, sink against their skin.

My mind went fuzzy. Warm. Like sinking into a bath...

The connection snapped into place. They were both there, in my mind, warm and sexy and perfect.

I reached up to the single button at the top of one shoulder. That button held everything in place.

I undid the button, let my dress fall to the floor.

I had another fabulous piece of lingerie beneath. This time I'd gone for all black. Thought it looked better with the thigh holster.

"Fuck." Zarren's need to claim me was hot and instant. Primal. More than sex, this would cement our future, make sure we would never be separated again.

Oberon's desire was so different. Not a lightning strike, like Zarren's. A slow burn, like lava rolling through his body to his cock.

Zarren was undressed first and was rewarded appropriately when I sank to my knees and sucked his hard length in my mouth.

His groan made Oberon move faster, the white-hot pull of my lips around his cock filled all of our minds.

My pussy clenched, wet and empty. Achy.

Zarren lifted me completely and pressed me to his chest. "Mine."

Oh, yes. Yes. Yes. Yes.

I lifted my legs and placed my ankles up over his hips. "Do it. Fuck me right here."

Standing up, in the middle of the living area, as Oberon stepped behind me, his hands cupping my ass.

This was what I'd been wanting, waiting for. This was what I needed. Both of them. Surrounding me. Touching me. Consuming my mind and my body until there wasn't room for anything else.

"You are not ready."

I rubbed my pussy over the top of Zarren's cock. He groaned. "Gods, female. We are supposed to pleasure you, not—"

I shifted my hips, my pussy sliding down to envelope him like a greedy little wench.

I leaned back, my side pressed to Oberon's chest. He kissed me. Consumed me.

Everything was in that kiss. Love. Devotion. Fear. Need.

Exposed. Every emotion, desire and ache laid bare.

"Do your magic thing. Make me ready. I want both of you." I filled my mind with what I wanted. Zarren's cock stretching my pussy, thrusting deep and fast. Oberon's cock in my ass, tight, aching, pushing me over the edge.

I didn't know which one of them activated the implant in my ass, didn't care as the warm lubricant filled me, prepared my body for this—for claiming my mates.

Zarren's gaze locked on my face, studied every blush and sigh and moan as Oberon worked his way inside. Carefully. A bit at a time until we stood locked together, all three of us, finally one.

Oberon rolled my nipples with his fingers. My pussy clenched around Zarren's cock.

Oberon groaned. "Fuck."

I used the muscles on my backside to squeeze Oberon's cock.

Zarren shuddered. "Gods, female."

This is going to be fun.

So naughty.

You like naughty, remember?

Yes. Yes, I did.

A SPECIAL THANK YOU TO MY READERS...

Want more? I've got *hidden* bonus content on my web site *exclusively* for those on my mailing list.

If you are already on my email list, you don't need to do a thing! Simply scroll to the bottom of my newsletter emails and click on the *super-secret* link.

Not a member? What are you waiting for? In addition to bonus content (great new stuff will be added regularly) you will always be in the loop - you'll never have to wonder when my newest release will hit the stores—AND you will get a free book as a special welcome gift.

Sign up now! http://freescifiromance.com

FIND YOUR INTERSTELLAR MATCH!

YOUR mate is out there. Take the test today and discover your perfect match. Are you ready for a sexy alien mate (or two)?

VOLUNTEER NOW!

interstellarbridesprogram.com

DO YOU LOVE AUDIOBOOKS?

Grace Goodwin's books are now available as audiobooks...everywhere.

LET'S TALK!

Interested in joining my **Sci-Fi Squad**? Meet new like-minded sci-fi romance fanatics and chat with Grace! Be part of a private Facebook group that shares pictures and fun news! Join here:

https://www.facebook.com/groups/scifisquad/

BE A SCI-FI SQUAD MEMBER

Want to talk about Grace Goodwin books with others? Join the **SPOILER ROOM** and spoil away! Your GG BFFs are waiting! (And so is Grace) Join here:

https://www.facebook.com/groups/ggspoilerroom/

JOIN THE GG SPOILER ROOM

GET A FREE BOOK!

JOIN MY MAILING LIST TO BE THE FIRST TO KNOW OF NEW RELEASES, FREE BOOKS, SPECIAL PRICES AND OTHER AUTHOR GIVEAWAYS.

http://freescifiromance.com

ALSO BY GRACE GOODWIN

Interstellar Brides® Program

Assigned a Mate

Mated to the Warriors

Claimed by Her Mates

Taken by Her Mates

Mated to the Beast

Mastered by Her Mates

Tamed by the Beast

Mated to the Vikens

Her Mate's Secret Baby

Mating Fever

Her Viken Mates

Fighting For Their Mate

Her Rogue Mates

Claimed By The Vikens

The Commanders' Mate

Matched and Mated

Hunted

Viken Command

The Rebel and the Rogue

Rebel Mate

Surprise Mates

Rogue Enforcer

Chosen by the Vikens

Marked Mate

Interstellar Brides® Program Boxed Set - Books 6-8

Interstellar Brides® Program Boxed Set - Books 9-12

Interstellar Brides® Program Boxed Set - Books 13-16

Interstellar Brides® Program Boxed Set - Books 17-20

Interstellar Brides® Program Boxed Set - Books 21-24

Bad Boys of Rogue 5

Interstellar Brides® Program: The Colony

Surrender to the Cyborgs

Mated to the Cyborgs

Cyborg Seduction

Her Cyborg Beast

Cyborg Fever

Rogue Cyborg

Cyborg's Secret Baby

Her Cyborg Warriors

Claimed by the Cyborgs

The Colony Boxed Set 1

The Colony Boxed Set 2

The Colony Boxed Set 3

Interstellar Brides® Program: The Virgins

The Alien's Mate

His Virgin Mate

Claiming His Virgin

His Virgin Bride

His Virgin Princess

The Virgins - Complete Boxed Set

Interstellar Brides® Program: Ascension Saga

Ascension Saga, book 1

Ascension Saga, book 2

Ascension Saga, book 3

Trinity: Ascension Saga - Volume 1

Ascension Saga, book 4

Ascension Saga, book 5

Ascension Saga, book 6

Faith: Ascension Saga - Volume 2

Ascension Saga, book 7

Ascension Saga, book 8

Ascension Saga, book 9

Destiny: Ascension Saga - Volume 3

Interstellar Brides® Program: The Beasts

Bachelor Beast

Maid for the Beast

Beauty and the Beast

The Beasts Boxed Set - Books 1-3

Big Bad Beast

Beast Charming

Bargain with a Beast

The Beasts Boxed Set - Books 4-6

Beast's Secret Baby

Starfighter Training Academy

The First Starfighter

Starfighter Command

Elite Starfighter

Starfighter Training Academy Boxed Set

Other Books

Dragon Chains

Their Conquered Bride

Wild Wolf Claiming: A Howl's Romance

SUBSCRIBE TODAY!

PATREON

Hi there! Grace Goodwin here. I am SO excited to invite you into my intense, crazy, sexy, romantic, imagination and the worlds born as a result. From Battlegroup Karter to The Colony and on behalf of the entire Coalition Fleet of Planets, I welcome you! Visit my Patreon page for additional bonus content, sneak peaks, and insider information on upcoming books as well as the opportunity to receive NEW RELEASE BOOKS before anyone else! See you there! ~ Grace

Grace's PATREON: https://www.patreon.com/gracegoodwin

ABOUT GRACE

Grace Goodwin is a USA Today and international bestselling author of Sci-Fi and Paranormal romance with over a million books sold. Grace's titles are available worldwide on all retailers, in multiple languages, and in ebook, print, audio and other reading App formats.

Grace is a full-time writer whose earliest movie memories are of Luke Skywalker, Han Solo, and real, working light sabers. (Still waiting for Santa to come through on that one.) Now Grace writes sexy-as-hell sci-fi romance six days a week. In her spare time, she reads, watches campy sci-fi and enjoys spending time with family and friends. No matter where she is, there is always a part of her dreaming up new worlds and exciting characters for her next book.

Grace loves to chat with readers and can frequently be found lurking in her Facebook groups. Interested in joining her **Sci-Fi Squad**? Meet new like-minded sci-fi romance fanatics and chat with Grace! Join here: https://www.facebook.com/groups/scifisquad/

Want to talk about Grace Goodwin books with others? Join the **SPOILER ROOM** and spoil away! Your GG BFFs are waiting! (And so is Grace) Join here:

https://www.facebook.com/groups/ggspoilerroom/

Printed in Great Britain
by Amazon